意林

公元787年，唐封疆大吏马总集诸子精华，编著成《意林》一书6卷，流传至今

意林：始于公元787年，距今1200余年

U0893085

彩英绘文

chicken soup for the soul

最 好 的 爱 是 陪 伴

意林

彩绘英文

忽然青春，一别经年

After Long Year

If I Should See You

《意林·绘英语》编辑部——编

吉林摄影出版社
·长春·

图书在版编目（CIP）数据

忽然青春，一别经年：汉、英 /《意林·绘英语》编辑部编绘. -- 长春：吉林摄影出版社, 2018.5
（彩绘英文）
ISBN 978-7-5498-3565-2

Ⅰ.①忽… Ⅱ.①意… Ⅲ.①故事—作品集—世界—汉、英 Ⅳ.①I14

中国版本图书馆CIP数据核字(2018)第074072号

忽然青春，一别经年 HURAN QINGCHUN YIBIEJINGNIAN

项目出品 意林彩绘英文
出版人 孙洪军
主编 顾平 杜普洲
责任编辑 施岚 孙瑜
总策划 蔡燕
丛书统筹 赵添天
策划编辑 赵添天 赵滢
执行编辑 赵滢
设计总监 资源
封面设计 徐丹
美术编辑 徐丹
开本 16.6mm×24mm 1/16
字数 200千字
印张 12
版次 2018年6月第1版
印次 2018年6月第1次印刷

出版 吉林摄影出版社
发行 吉林摄影出版社
地址 长春市泰来街1825号
邮编：130062
电话 总编办：0431-86012616
发行科：0431-86012602
网址 www.jlsycbs.net
经销 全国各地新华书店
印刷 小森印刷（北京）有限公司

书号 ISBN 978-7-5498-3565-2 定价：36.90元

启事

本书编选时参阅了部分报刊和著作，我们未能与部分作品的文字作者、漫画作者以及插画作者取得联系，在此深表歉意。请各位作者见到本书后及时与我们联系，以便按国家相关规定支付稿酬及赠送样书。

地址：北京市朝阳区南磨房路37号华腾北搪商务大厦1501室《意林》编辑部（100022）

电话：010-51900482

目录 contents

第1章：嗨，女孩，你很美

第2章：我不是胖，只是灵魂比较大

第3章：写给食物的情书

第 4 章：走在我身边，做我的朋友

第5章：成长路上，全新的冒险

第1章 嗨，女孩，你很美

Hey Girl, You Are Beautiful

（文◎ Gerard Way）

Hey, girls, you're beautiful. Don't look at those stupid magazines with sticklike models. Eat healthy and exercise. That's all. Don't let anyone tell you you're not good enough. You're good enough, you are too good. Love your family with all your heart and listen to it. You are gorgeous, whether you're a size 4 or 14. It doesn't matter what you look like on the outside, as long as you're a good person, as long as you respect others. I know it's been told hundreds of times before, but it's true. Hey, girls, you are beautiful.

嗨，女孩，你很美

（文◎杰拉德·威）

嗨，女孩，你很漂亮。不要学那些鬼杂志上瘦得像杆儿一样的模特。好好吃饭，经常运动，这就够了。不要听别人说你还不够好。你绝对够好，你真的非常好。用心爱你的家人，倾听自己内心的声音。不管你是穿 4 号还是穿 14 号衣服，你都很美。只要你善良、尊重他人，颜值和外形就显得不那么重要了。我知道这个道理被人讲了无数遍，但事实的确是这样的。嗨，女孩，你很漂亮。绘英语

What if I Grow Up With the Red

(文◎ Nathan Harris)

At some point in the past year I deceloped a habit of avoiding mirrors. It was gradual and subconscious, but eventually it rooted itself in my mind.

Ultimately. I had an encounter with my reflection while washing my hands in a restau rantbathroom. It became apparent then what had driven me away from looking at myself...I had The Reds.

Some might refer to The Reds as pimples or acne,but mine were not your pimples;what I was dealing with here were erupting lumps of fleshlaming red. While other kids were popping exits after a week,I was, nursing mine to "calm down a bit",as my mother put it. The chance of them actually disappearing was almost laughable; my only hope was that they might just take it" down a notch" and level out to where my forehead skin usually rests.

Looking at myself in the restroom mirror only confirmed what I should have accepted long ago. My brothers had already taken up the duty of attacking me with comments such as "Oh,I see Mt. Kilimanjaro is peaking mighty high up there on your forehead". How funny. Soon enough my forehead hosted what appeared to be the world's highest mo untains:Everest,Kanchenjunga,McKinly. Each had spot on my face to call its own,somewhere deep down,I felt as if l had a vested interest in each and everyone of them. If I was going to endure comments about how I should wash my face and quit eating greasy foods (which, l might note,

does not stop acne). At least I could become a bit more intimate with the temporary guests on my forehead.

I found myself staring at each pimple in the morning, mentally recording its growth and even applauding its development. I applauded more, of course, if it decreased its size in some rare but laudable act. Either way, friends and strangers were always willing to lend their tips and support. It was as if the citizens of my town had become overnight experts on dermatology. They spoke in a coy and indirect manner as if to avoid hurting feelings or sounding cruel: "What do you know about witch hazel? I hear it does wonders for skin. Not that I'm saying you should use it, just telling you what I heard."

What they didn't understand was that The Reds are like some sort of advanced tuberculosis, resistant to drugs, able to change and thrive in any

environment. The Reds don't just react to skincare products. They act. If I ever did find an effective face wash,I soon realized that focusing on my forehead only caused a new flare-up on my cheek. Focus on scraping the face wash on my cheek,and the corner of my lip would bulge with a red welt, bigger than any I'd ever seen. When I thought I had my whole face covered,bumps formed beneath my eyebrows. The Reds were innovative agents of change,willing to go wherever a temporarily potent face wash forced them to go.

Sometimes I thought about my dad's situation. Before I was born,he developed skin cancer,which was successfully removed during a long,drawn—out surgery. Unfortunately,the procedure left him with a massive scar across his cheek. Of course. I never paid any attention to it,living with him and all,but in large crowds,he drew stares. A conversation with someone and you would soon notice that person listening to him while subconsciously itching or rubbing the side of their face,a constant reminder as to where their mind really was in the exchange on a smaller scale,I noticed the same traits in people encountered. While we started out speaking eye to eye,we ended up speaking eye to forehead,their gaze getting higher and higher.

Mentioning it only made things that much more awkward. It left me feeling less than human, knowing that my body—my face—was more important than who I was altogether.

But like many teen centered issues, The Reds would eventually disappear. From Mt. Kilimanjaroon, each mountain toppled over. Some would leave scars from my constant scratching and squeezing, while others departed in a quieter manner, as if they had never erupted in the first place. Either way, I gradually settled with the embarrassment and grief I carried in my own face. The Reds or not, I decided I wouldn't let them keep me from enjoying the life I wanted to lead.

I think back to a trip to Universal Studios with my dad. We sat at a table finishing lunch before we headed toward another line for a ride. He ate casually, but between bites it seemed as if I were the only one aware of the visitors who happened to walk by and make note of his cheek. I leaned in to Dad and expressed my concern, "I really wish they wouldn't stare like that. What's their problem?" He barely glanced up from his food as he issued his response, "Who cares? I know I don't, that much is certain. Let hem stare. I learned that lesson a long time ago."

Such simple wisdom hit me deep in my heart of hearts. He wasn't about to let anyone influence how he felt at the given moment. He's got a scar... and it doesn't even matter. not to him at least. Maybe to the people walking by it did, but to him? Not a chance. When we finished eating, we proceeded to have the time of our lives. Be it my forehead or his cheek, some would gawk others would gape, but I can say with the utmost sincerity that we were the Last to notice, and the Last to care.

就算长痘又何妨

（文◎南森·哈里斯 译◎光辉）

从去年的某个时候开始，我逐渐养成了不愿照镜子的习惯。这个习惯起初是无意识慢慢形成的，但最终在我的脑海里扎了根。

终于有一天，当我在一家餐厅的洗手间洗手时，我无意中看到了镜中的自己。令我一直无法直视自己的原因这下子清楚了——我长了大红包。

有的人也许会把这些大红包叫作粉刺或痤疮，不过，我长的这些包可跟你们一般人长的不一样。我要对付的是突然大批冒出的肿块，而且它们居然是鲜红色的。当别的孩子一周后就能把脓包挤掉时，我的包在我的精心照顾之下只是变得——用我妈妈的话说——“平静了一些”。想让它们真正消失几乎是个笑话，我唯一的希望是它们可以“稍加收敛一下”，恢复到我的额头皮肤本来的高度。

看着洗手间镜子里的自己只是证实了我早就该承认的事实。我的兄弟们早已将打击我视为己任，比如他们会评论说：“嗬，我看见乞力马扎罗山在你的脑门儿上冒得好高好高啊。”真好笑。没用多久，我的脑门儿上看起来就好像是世界高峰都来安家了一样，有珠穆朗玛峰、干城章嘉峰、麦金利（又名德纳里山）。每座高峰都在我的脸上有自己名下的一个包。在我心底的某个角落，我觉得自己似乎跟这些包中的每一个都息息相关。对于我该怎么洗脸以及戒掉油腻食品这类的意见（我要指出，这么做并不能预防痘痘），如果我打算去忍受，那对脑门儿上的这些临时访客我至少可以表现得更亲近一点儿。

我发现自己会在早上端详每一个痘痘，并在心里记下它们的生长状况，甚至为它们的长势叫好。当然，如果它们难得变小了一点儿（这令人称道），我会更加大声叫好。不管怎样，朋友们和陌生人都乐意为我提供他们的小窍门，送上他们的支持。仿佛我们镇上的居民一夜之间都摇身一变成了皮肤专家。他们忸怩而婉转地对我说（好像是为了避免伤害我的感情或避免让自己显得太冷酷似的）：“你对金缕梅酊剂了解不？我听说它对皮肤问题有奇效。我可不是说你应该用它，只是告诉你我听说的。”

他们不明白的是，这些大红包就像是某种晚期结核病一样，具有抗药性，能够变化，并可以在任何环境下茁壮成长。对于护肤产品，这些大红包不只是做出反应，它们会采取行动。即使我真的找到了一种管用的洗面乳，我也很快就会发现，把精力全部放在脑门儿上只会导致我的脸上突然泛起一片新的红包。我忙着用洗面乳使劲去洗脸，可嘴角上又会肿起一个大到前所未见的红疙瘩。当我以为自己已经把脸上的每个地方都照顾到时，我的眉毛下边又鼓起了一堆肿包。这些大红包富于创新、灵活善变，愿意前往暂时见效的洗面乳将它们驱往的任何地方。

有时我会想到爸爸的情况。他在我出生之前得了皮肤癌，经过一次极其漫长的手术，病灶被成功切除了。遗憾的是，那次手术在他脸上留下了一道大大的伤疤。当然，由于我们一直生活在一起，我从来不会留意他的伤疤，但是在人多的地方，他总会引来旁人的目光。当他跟别人说话时，你很快就会发现，对方一边在听他讲话，一边在下意识地挠挠或是蹭蹭自己的脸，这个动作时刻提醒着你，他们的心思在谈话过程中其实在哪里。我在我遇到的那些人身上也发现了同样的特征，虽然表现得没有那么明显。谈话伊始，我们还能看着彼此的眼睛，可是他们的目光渐渐上移，聊到最后，眼睛就盯在我的脑门儿上了。

提及这一点只会让场面变得越发尴尬。发现我的身体，我的脸，比我整个人还要重要，这让我感觉自己低人一等。

不过，和许多主要发生在青少年身上的问题一样，大红包最终也会退去。从“乞力马扎罗山”包开始，每

座“峰”包都倒下了。有一些包会因为我经常挠、经常挤而留下疤痕，另一些在离去时则更加悄无声息，仿佛它们从来就没有出来过一样。不管怎样，我渐渐地与我的脸带给我的尴尬和难过达成了和解。不管是大红包还是别的什么，我决意不让它们阻挡我去享受自己想要过的那种生活。

我想起了跟爸爸一起去环球影城游玩的那次经历。在前去排队等候玩下一处游乐设施前，我们坐在一张餐桌旁吃午饭。他漫不经心地吃着，但在这期间，仿佛只有我注意到了当那些游客恰好从我们身边经过时，他们会留意爸爸的脸颊。我朝爸爸探过身去，表达了我的关心：“我真希望他们别那么盯着你看。他们是不是有毛病啊？”爸爸几乎都没有将视线从他的食物上抬高一点儿，就发出了自己的回应：“谁在乎呢？反正我知道我不在乎。让他们盯着去吧。我早就把这种事儿想明白了。”

如此朴素的智慧令我的内心深感震撼。他不打算让任何人影响到他在某一时刻的心情。他有道疤……但那根本无关紧要，至少对他而言是这样的。也许对那些从他身旁经过的人来说这件事很重要，可对他而言完全没有这种可能。吃完饭后，我们继续尽情享受快乐的时光。无论是我的脑门儿还是他的脸颊，有的人会呆头呆脑地盯着看，有的人会目瞪口呆地注视着，不过我可以以最真诚的态度说，我们自己根本没注意，也根本不在意。

What Is It Like to Be an Attractive Woman

(文◎ Vinati Singh)

Two years ago I fell off the steps of a bus while climbing down and twisted my ankle. What followed was the usual procedure that is common in the US. The EMT's came almost immediately and I was loaded on to an ambulance and taken to a hospital. A few hours later I was treated and discharged.

What was uncommon was how I was treated while going to ER and while I was in the hospital. People were kind to me, men and women alike. They even went the extra mile that they didn't have to. They wheeled me into a private room instead of making me wait in the crowded ER waiting room. Someone came and asked me if the temperature was okay and if I need the AC adjusted. When I said I was cold, he brought me a blanket and some magazines, in case I got bored. The nurses stopped by, making pleasant chitchat with me. Random people asked me if I was in too much pain, did I need anything... etc. There were other people who were brought in while I was waiting. Old patients groaning in pain were given the provisions they needed and then ignored. A woman who's face was bitten severely by an Akita was left in a corner holding wads of tissue to her face while howling in pain. Nobody was abandoned without treatment but it was obvious to me that others (mostly the elderly, the infirm, the seemingly unattractive) were treated clinically and ticked off the "to do" charts. A sprained ankle is not priority, so while I was not pushed to the front of the line, my stay was made as pleasant as possible. Why would people do that? ER staff, who understand what real pain is like, certainly knew I didn't need their attention like others did. Why were others treated clinically while I got coddled? Others got more care, but I got kindness.

My mother had a stroke 17 years ago and has had several mini strokes since then. I have made many trips to ER with her. This story doesn't change. It broke my heart that night to see the contrast that I was treated with compared to what I watch my mother go through every couple of years. I came home from ER that day and wept silently, after seeing first hand how differently I got treated versus the people who really needed it. People like my mother, whom the world ignores. Nobody acknowledges the pain, the struggle, the helplessness of the less fortunate.

So do I enjoy it? Every day. Without realizing it. Like any other good looking, healthy, independent person, man or woman. As second nature. The world is just nicer to attractive people. Just like the world is nicer to rich people. I'm not in the dating world. It's not about free drinks, gifts and luxuries. It's about people being nice. Smiling at you when you're having a bad day. Showing a little extra care in dealing with you. The politeness, the attention, the little niceties. It's a privilege and I don't take it lightly.

There are no real problems associated with being an attractive woman that any other woman would not face anyway. The attention from men is fine when it's positive. The cat calling, the brashness and the threatening nature of male attention doesn't come from aesthetic appreciation. It comes from a place of aggression and all women and even young girls learn this early in life.

The attention does feel shallow at times. It certainly did in that ER room. But who am I to turn away people who in their minds are just being nice? Do they go through a mental calculation of exactly how much niceness my degree of beauty deserves? Of course not. And the flip side is a lot worse. I'm grateful for any positive behavior because I know this is temporary. Eventually I will join the ranks of the elderly, the infirm and the seemingly unattractive.

One thing I refuse to do is to make excuses for being attractive. I know it's subjective and I know it's temporary. I know it's the luck of the draw and I know that I'm just one of many. I know it means nothing in the long run and I know it means a lot for first impressions. So I refuse to go Anon for fear of seeming immodest. I don't control it anymore than I control any other invariable factor in my life. It means nothing to the people who are truly important to me. Does it matter to my husband or my mother or my kids what I look like? When I'm sitting and chatting with my friends do we care what the other person looks like? No. And I wouldn't have it any other way. But I also won't disrespect this privilege by pretending it doesn't exist.

女性颜值高是一种怎样的体验

（文◎维娜娣·辛格　译◎周然）

两年前一次下公交车时，我跌下了台阶，扭伤了脚踝。紧随其后的是一套美国式的常规流程。紧急医疗救护人员在第一时间赶到，将我抬上救护车，赶往医院。几个小时后，我接受了治疗，随后便出院了。

故事的不寻常之处在于，无论是在去往急诊室的路上还是在医院时，我都受到了诸多关照。男男女女都对我友善备至。他们本不必大费周章。他们推着我的轮椅进了单人病房，这样我就不必等在拥挤的候诊室了。有人过来问我房内的温度是否适宜，是否需要调节空调的温度。我说有点儿冷，他就给我拿了条毯子，怕我觉得无聊，他还带来了杂志。护士们停下来与我亲切交谈。不断有人过来问我疼不疼，问我是否需要什么帮助，等等。在我等候的时候，还有其他病患被送进了医院。年长的病患痛苦呻吟，在得到最基本的治疗后就被晾在了一边；一个被秋田犬严重咬伤面部的女人将纸巾敷在脸上痛苦哀号，却被留在了角落里。所有病患都得到了救治，但我分明感到，他们（大部分是年长者、虚弱者、相貌平平者）被草草对待，列入了“已完成”的清单中。脚踝扭伤并不需要得到优先治疗，尽管我没有被安排到队伍前列，他们带给我的就诊体验却好得不能再好了。为什么人们会这样做？急诊室人员明白什么是真正的疼痛，也显然知道我并不像其他病患那样需要关照。可为什么其他人被敷衍了事，我却被呵护有加？其他人所得到的只是治疗，我却收获了善意。

十七年前，我妈妈患了脑卒中，从那时起，她的脑卒中发作了好几次。我陪她去过许多次急诊室，因此看到了故事的另一面。那天晚上，想到我所受到的关照，再对比这些年来我妈妈经受的，我的心都碎了。从急诊室回家的那个晚上，在亲眼目睹我和那些真正需要帮助的病患所受到的不同关照后，我默默地哭了。这个世界忽视了那些像我妈妈一样的人。没有人在意这些相貌平平者的疼痛、挣扎和无助。

我享受吗？每一天，不自知地。就像任何一名好看、健康、独立的男性或者女性一样。这个世界对颜值高的人更和善，这已经成了一种第二本能。我不是单指约会时，它无关免费酒水、礼物和奢侈品。它关乎人们的善意：当你过了糟糕的一天，人们朝你微笑；与你相处时，他们会多表达一些关心。可这并不是我理应获得的特权。

颜值高的女性要面对一些其他女性无须面对的困扰，不过，这倒没什么问题。如果男性的关注是善意的，则无可非议。但他们的口哨、盛气凌人、震慑，并不出于审美欣赏。它出于一种侵略，这是所有女性，甚至连年轻女孩们，都早已认清的。

有时候，这种关注让人感到肤浅。急诊室里的关注便是如此。但我又凭什么拒绝这些出于善意的人呢？难道他们精确计算过我的美貌值多少善意？当然没有。事情的另一面更糟了。我对一切善举都心怀感激，因为它们不是长久的。终有一天，我也将变得年迈、体弱与相貌平平。

我拒绝依仗自己的美貌找借口。我知道它是主观的，也是短暂的。我知道美貌是种运气，何况世上貌美之人不在少数。我知道在漫漫人生路中它无关紧要，尽管它确实对第一印象的建立有很大影响。我从不匿名答题，生怕显得傲慢。生活中的定数我无以掌控，颜值更是如此。对于那些对我重要的人来说，它毫不重要。对于我的丈夫、母亲或者孩子而言，我的颜值重要吗？与朋友喝茶聊天时，我们会在意他们的颜值吗？不会，我不会这样。但是，我也不会装作漠视这种特权的存在，因为这种做法本身便是对它的蔑视。

This Is How Easy It Is For You To Be Ugly

（文◎ Alden Tan ）

You know, I've dated a bunch of pretty girls before. Some of them are hot even, being models and all.

I was enamored by them. I'll admit it. I like my women pretty.

But then it made me realize that looks can only get you so far, for the very fact that it's extremely easy to turn ugly.

When you're drunk, you're ugly. No one wants to see that. In this case, no one wants to smell that alcohol on you.

When you're angry, you're ugly. Your face is frowning. Your eyebrows are creased. You give off this angry vibe which people can detect a mile away. People can get scared even.

When you're mad and spewing profanities needlessly from your mouth, you're ugly. No one wants to hear that .

When you're sad and crying hysterically, you're ugly. It shows you can't control your emotions and that you love drama.

When you're shouting, you're ugly. It's loud, rude, annoying and very barbaric.

When you're disrespectful towards others, say the cashier or cab driver, you're ugly. It's mean and shows what kind of person you really are.

Way too many people are putting good looking people on a pedestal. Then we judge them to be good people because we're attracted to them.

We think that looking good is some feature that is blessed on a lucky few on this planet. We think that they have it all and got an edge in life that

the less attractive people here don't get.

But that's all meaningless. They can turn ugly anytime.

That is why ultimately, character and personality count for a lot, if not for everything.

There's really no reason to be so taken in by people who look good unless you get to know them for who they are.

I can't say I've not been guilty in several of the offences above. I know I look good, that much I'm confident in. But I've been ugly many times before, especially when I get angry.

Heck, imagine how ugly I was when I was younger, when it comes to talking to girls and looking like a boyband wanna be popstar. So it's not about looking good. It never was. Destroy that pedestal.

If you can't back it up with a good attitude, character, values and respect for others, then your looks are useless. If you do continue to attract people with bad character altogether, then you're attracting the wrong people who only see you from the outside, and that'll never make you happy.

If you want to beautiful, then be happy. Happiness inspires. That's real beauty.

要变丑有多容易

（文◎奥尔登·坦 译◎丁仔）

你知道，我以前也约过一些漂亮女孩。有一些很漂亮，是做模特之类工作的。

我承认，我为这样的女孩倾倒，我喜欢我的女人漂漂亮亮的。

可我又想，长相也只能帮你这么多了，因为人极易变丑。

你要是喝得烂醉如泥，那就丑大了！没人想看你那副样子，闻你身上那股酒臭。

你要是生气了，也会变丑。你的脸啊，皱起来，眉头紧锁，这团怨恨的小宇宙能拒人千里之外，让人只想躲得远远的。

你气急败坏的时候，无意义地乱飙脏话，你很丑！没人想听这些鬼话。

你悲伤欲绝，哭得死去活来时，你很丑！这说明你无法控制自己的感情，情绪反复无常。

你乱喊乱叫时，也很丑！太吵了，粗鲁，烦人，没教养。

你不尊重别人时，比如说，对收银员、的士司机，你也很丑！这太小气了，也说明了你是什么样的人。

非常多的人把好看的人放在神坛上，给他们贴上好人的标签，就因为他们很养眼。

我们会觉得长得好看是老天给少数人的恩赐。我们认为帅哥美女们拥有了全部，比长相平庸的人有更多优势。

这毫无意义。他们随时都会变丑。

这便是为什么，到最后性格和人品会那么重要，即便不是在所有事上。

除非你认识这些长得好看的人，了解他们，否则你没有什么理由那么看好他们。

我为以上的叙述和冒犯负有罪恶感。我知道自己长得好看，因此得到很多自信。但我也丑过无数次，特别是我生气的时候。

天哪，你知道我年轻的时候有多丑吗？那时什么都不懂，跟女孩子说话的时候，假装自己是男生组合的偶像。所以关键从来不在于是否长得好看，别再神化外表的重要性。

如果你不能用好的态度、性格、价值观和对别人的尊重作为支撑，那么你的外表定会黯然失色。如果你用糟糕的性格配上美丽的容颜来吸引别人，那么你招来的只会是错的人，他们只看得到你的外在，这不会使你真正快乐的。

如果你想变美，那么开心一点儿，那才是真正的美丽。

I Have 50,0000 Fans, *but This Life Is Untruthful*

（文◎ Essena O'Neil）

There is nothing zen about tying to look zen. Taking a photo of you trying to be zen and proving your zen on instagram.

A 15 year old girl that calorie restricts and excessively exercises is not goals. Anyone addicted to social media fame like I once was, is no [sic] in a conscious state.

Please like this photo, I put on makeup, curled my hair, tight dress, big uncomfortable jewellery... Took over 50 shots until I got one I thought you might like, then I edited this one selfie for ages on several apps, just so I could feel some social approval from you.

No purpose in a forced smile. Tiny clothes and being paid to look pretty. We are a generation told to consume and consume, with no thought of where it all comes from and where it all goes.

I didn't pay for the dress, took countless photos trying to look hot for instagram, the formal made me feel incredibly alone.

"I'm the girl that 'had it all' and I want to tell you that 'having it all'on social media means absolutely nothing to your real life... I let myself be defined by numbers and the only thing that made me feel better about myself ... really was the more followers, the more likes, the more praise and the more views I got online. It was never enough..."

After all, social media can have a positive influence on you, if you consume it in moderation.

Either way, may you stay true and find your inner peace!

我有 50 万粉丝，但这种生活不真实

（文◎艾森娜·奥尼尔）

Essena O'Neill，澳大利亚的一位平面模特，今年只有 18 岁。她笑容甜美，身材婀娜，跟绝大多数同龄人一样，喜欢晒自己的日常照和美照。

她在Instagram（国外照片分享网站）上积累了50多万粉丝，在YouTube（油管视频）上有25万订阅者，应该可以称为一呼万应的“网红（social media celebrity）”了。

从高中开始使用社交媒体到现在，女孩接到的代言越来越多，18岁就已经可以赚钱养家了。

可就在这两天，女孩突然在她2000多张的Instagram美照里，写下拍照时的真实情况。

看起来颇有禅意，但是在Ins上拍照故意表现禅意的时候一点儿禅意也没有。

严控卡路里还有大量的运动不应该是15岁女孩的目标。任何一个像我曾经那样沉迷于社交媒体的人都不够清醒。

请为这张照片点赞，我化上妆，烫了头发，穿着紧身的衣服，戴着大而不适的首饰……从50多张照片里才挑出这张我觉得你们会喜欢的照片，然后花了大量时间在不同的手机应用上编辑这张自拍，就是为了得到你们的赞美。

毫无意义地勉强微笑。别人掏钱，我只负责把小得不能再小的衣服穿得好看。我们这一代已被洗脑，成天就是消费、消费，从来不想何去何从。

这条裙子不是我买的，为了图片性感而拍了无数张照片。可穿着这样的服饰，我感到无比孤独。

“我是你们眼里‘什么都有’的女孩，但我想告诉你们的是，在社交媒体上拥有一切，对你的现实生活毫无益处。这之前，我活的就像是一组数据，也只有数据能让我感觉舒服一些……我在网上有了越来越多的粉丝和更多的‘赞’，还有更多的褒奖和评论。但是内心好像永远都不会满足……”

不过社交媒体可能也会对你有积极的影响，只要你能掌握好一个度。

无论怎样，希望你能保有真实的自己，找到内心的平静。

绘英语

Choose for Yourself What Your Reality Will Be

（文◎ Anonymous）

I remember an instance when I was probably 10 and my mother told me I had a boogerin my nose. She told me out of kindness before leaving the house but still I felt crushed. This simple instance has stuck with me. I let it grow into being by watering it with my fear and thoughts of not being good enough，an embarrassment，even ugly.

No more. I will not allow this seed to grow any longer. I will take responsibility for my thoughts and not put the responsibility or blame on others. I choose my thoughts. I choose how I feel about myself.

But what if there is someone in your life actually telling you that you are fat or ugly or a failure?

You are still responsible for making those sayings a reality. You can choose to make them a reality or you can squash them immediately and not let them ever enter your thought.

Taking control of your thoughts is huge. Once you become aware that every thought you have the good，the bad and the ugly is a choice then you can take the steps to choose to only allow the good into your consciousness and therefore your reality.

First off，simply by becoming conscious of your thoughts. Take note of your thoughts throughout the day.

When you look in the mirror，what are your thoughts saying? Where did they come from? Are you going to choose to water those thoughts? Are there new thoughts you are willing to replace with the old?

Taking control and responsibility for your thoughts will set you on a path of conscious control of your direction in life.

Stop allowing other people to take the lead. Choose for yourself what your reality will be.

为你将要成为的现实做出选择

（文◎佚名）

我记得曾经在我十岁左右，我母亲告诉我鼻子中有鼻屎。她在出门前善意地将这告知于我，可我仍然感到崩溃。我一直为这件小事纠结着。我任它发展成恐惧、自我感觉不够好、尴尬，甚至认为自己长得丑的想法。

到此为止吧！我不会再任其生长。我将对我的想法负责，不会把责任推给其他人或是责备他人。我选择拥有怎样的想法。我选择持有怎样的自我感觉。

可如果你生活中就是有人告诉你，你胖 / 丑 / 做人失败呢？

让这些言论成为事实的你仍须承担责任。你能选择让它们成真，也能立马将之粉碎，不把它们考虑在内。

控制住你的想法这事不简单。一旦你开始意识到你所秉持的每个想法是好、是坏还是丑陋取决于你的选择时，你要注意每个选择的步骤，只让好的想法进入你的意识，然后使之成为现实。

首先，只须意识到你的想法。全天候注意你的想法。

当你照镜子时，你的想法在说什么？它们从何而来？你是否会选择发展这些想法？你是否愿意用这些新的想法去代替之前的想法呢？

控制住你的想法，并对自己的想法负责，将会让你踏上有意识控制自己人生方向的道路。

别被其他人牵着鼻子走。为你将要成为的现实做出选择。

This Is a Letter from Your Much Older

(文◎ Anonymous)

Great.

Dear Lindsay.

Dear Lily.

Dear Bunny from long, long ago.

Dear me.

What's up?

This is a letter from your much older, cooler, better-dressed self.

I remember being you, and I remember it being really, really difficult.

You're worried about a lot of things right now.

The coarse black hair.

Your grades. Your body.

Falling in love.

Dating, your body.

The color of our skin.

Not feeling black enough.

You don't feel like you fit in anywhere now.

There was this one really mean girl, who would just bully me constantly.

Some of the people you thought were your friends are going to write mean things about you online.

The ones that push you around, and don't make time, and treat other people poorly.

I wish I could be like them.

But I wanted them to like me.

I wanted to be more like them.

And it was just silly, because...

All those amazing different qualities that you have no one else has.

Embrace them. Experience them.

Don't follow the crowd, and be who you want to be.

Stop trying so hard to be someone you're not.

Don't let anybody else...

Try to bring you down or make you second-guess yourself.

Stay who you're.

It's OK to be different. It doesn't make you a bad person.

There's not one person on the face of the planet who can replace you.

You're gonna meet a version of yourself that you never knew existed. So don't stress out too much about how you look or how cool you're.

Just go for it. Be unique. Yes!

I mean, look at you now: you're a huge weirdo. You're so different. People kind of like you.

To go ahead, and mess up big. Failure is not the end of the world.

Don't be afraid of being afraid.

Just be strong and be confident.

You are good enough.

You always have been.

You've got lots of energy, you're bursting with life.

And you can achieve whatever you want.

未来的你对自己说

（文◎佚名）

好！

亲爱的琳赛，

亲爱的莉莉，

亲爱的很久很久以前的邦妮，

亲爱的我，

你还好吗？

这是一封来自未来自己的信，她长大了，很酷，穿得也很靓。

我记得当年，那时过得非常非常痛苦。

你为各种琐事忧心忡忡。

粗糙的黑发，

成绩，体形，

恋爱，

约会，身材，

肤色。

会觉得自己举止不够像黑人。

自己与世界格格不入。

有个刻薄的姑娘，总是欺负我。

一些你视为好友的人，在网上诋毁你。

有人把你推来搡去，总是爽约，对人又差。

但我当时还希望别人都喜欢我，希望跟别人一样。

我希望自己跟别人相同。

这样想真蠢，因为……

你如此不同，如此优异，你和别人不同。

拥抱自己的特质，感受自己的不同。

不要随波逐流，想成为什么样的人，就做什么样的人。

不要再拼命成为别人。

不要允许任何人……

打垮你，或让你怀疑自己。

做自己。

与众不同没什么，不附和别人不意味着你是坏人。

在这颗星球上，你独一无二，无可取代。

你会成为意想不到的自己。所以啊，别压力太大，别总想着自己美不美、酷不酷。

加油争取。做独一无二的自己。加油！

我说，看看现在的你：超级怪胎啊。你非常独特，人们还都蛮喜欢你呢。

意气风发向前，轰轰烈烈做事。失败又不是世界末日。

胆小并不可耻。

做个强大而自信的人。

你非常优秀。

一直以来都是如此。

你充满能量，活力四射。

你心之所愿，无所不成。

People Who Are Totally Comfortable With Who They Are

(文◎ Anonymous)

I cherish being around people who are totally comfortable with who they are. There always seems to be an aura of love and acceptance that follows these folks around.

I think it's because they've figured out one of the biggest secrets to life: The possibility of being loved and accepted grows exponentially when we can truly say we couldn't be more comfortable with ourselves.

People like being around those who are comfortable with themselves because they're less threatening. We all feel the need to protect ourselves from threats aimed at our insecurities.

Insecurities are like open wounds, and it hurts when people poke at them.

It can be exhausting to hang around folks who constantly poke at us just to gain some kind of external validation through making everyone else feel smaller.

My favorite thing about people who are comfortable with themselves is they need no external validation.

They have discovered their worth is intrinsic and, by nature, something that cannot be taken away or added to based on what other people think.

Ironically enough, this ends up providing comfortable people with more external validation than those who feel they need it most.

Because comfortable people's worth comes from within, they see no point in tearing others down. To them, the only sensible way to speak about another is positively.

I guess when you realize your worth comes from within, you might as well build others up rather than tear them down, since their size is of no threat to your sense of self-worth.

Plus, it's a lot more fun to speak love to others and watch their eyes glow than it is to hurt someone's feelings for a cheap laugh, anyway.

When we become comfortable with ourselves through fully accepting who we are, we can silence the noise our insecurities make in public situations and become more attuned to the wonderful reality that unfolds before us.

The result is a world with fewer insecurities. To me, that sounds like a better world.

悦己者

（文◎佚名）

在我眼里，悦己的人非常可贵。他们身上总是闪耀着爱和接纳的光环。

我认为这是因为他们找到了一个生活最大的秘密：当我们能够真正悦己时，我们被爱和被接纳的可能性才会更大。

人们喜欢和悦己的人在一起，因为和他们在一起比较有安全感，而人都有远离威胁、打消不安全感的需求。

不安全感就像是裸露的伤口，只要碰了就会疼。

有些人就为了通过使别人觉得自己渺小而获得外界的某种认可，总是来戳我们的伤口。和这样的人待在一起，我们会筋疲力尽。

对于那些悦己的人，我很喜欢的一点就是他们不需要外界的认可。

他们已经发现自己的价值是内在的，是与生俱来的，不会被别人抢走，也不会因为别人的看法而增加。

讽刺的是，相较于那些非常渴望别人认可的人来说，悦己的人最终能得到更多的外界认可。

因为悦己的人的价值来自于内在，他们觉着诋毁别人没有意义。对他们而言，积极地谈论别人才是唯一明智的方式。

我想当你意识到你的价值来自内心的时候，你倒不如赞美别人，而不是诋毁他们，因为他们并不会威胁到你的自尊。

此外，对别人说出你的爱，看着他们眼里充满喜悦，这要比小气地嘲笑别人而伤害他们要更有趣。

当我们完全接受自己、完全悦己时，我们就能够使在公众场合产生的不安全感销声匿迹，也更能理解眼前的美好。

因此，世界上的不安全感就会减少，对我来说，那就是一个更美好的世界。

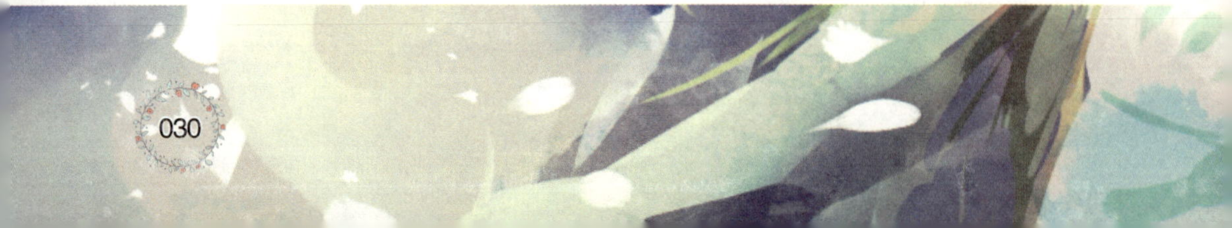

Mary,
I' m Glad I Have Chosen You

（文◎ Anonymous）

Mary:

The reason I forgive you is because you are not perfect.

You are imperfect, and so am I.

All humans are imperfect, even the man outside my apartment who litters.

When I was young, I wanted to be anybody but myself.

Dr Bernard Hazelhof said if I was on a desert island, then I would have to get used to my own company— just me and the coconuts.

He said I would have to accept myself, my warts and all, and that we don' t get to choose our warts.

They are a part of us and we have to live with them.

We can, however, choose our friends and I'm glad I have chosen you.

Dr Bernard Hazelhof also said that everyone's life is like a very long sidewalk.

Some are well paved. Others, like mine, have cracks, banana skins and cigarette butts.

Your sidewalk is like mine but probably not as many cracks.

Hopefully, one day our sidewalks will meet and we can share a can of condensed milk.

You are my best friend.

You are my only friend.

Max

玛丽，我很高兴选择了你

（文◎佚名）

玛丽：

我原谅你是因为你不是完美的。

你并不完美，而我也一样。

所有人都是不完美的，即便是那些在我公寓外面乱扔杂物的人。

我年轻的时候，想成为除了自己以外的任何一个人。

伯纳德·哈斯豪夫医生说，如果我在一座孤岛上，我就必须适应一个人生活，因为那里只有椰子和我。

他说我必须接受我自己，我的缺点和我的全部，因为我们无法选择自己的缺点。

它们是我们的一部分，我们必须要和它们一起活着。

然而，我们能选择我们的朋友，我很高兴选择了你。

伯纳德·哈斯豪夫医生还说，每个人的人生就是一条很长的人行道。

有的很平坦，而有的像我的一样，有裂缝、香蕉皮和烟头。

你的人行道和我的很像，但也许没有我的这么多裂缝。

有朝一日，希望你我的人行道会相会在一起，那时我们可以分享一罐炼乳。

你是我最好的朋友。

你是我唯一的朋友。

麦克斯 绘英语

A Postcard Addressed for Short-haired Girls

写给短发女孩的励志明信片

（文◎ Anonymous 佚名）

一个女孩捐掉长发后创作了这个 Shorter For Greater 明信片系列。

Beauty is only temporary, but your mind lasts you a lifetime.

—Alicia Machado

美貌只是暂时的，但你的思想会持续一生。

——艾丽西亚·马查朵（1996 年的环球小姐）

Beauty is whatever gives joy.

—Edna St. Vincent Millay

一切能带来愉悦的东西都是美的。

——埃德娜·文森特·默蕾（美国历史上第一位得到普利兹诗歌奖的女性）

Things are beautiful if you love them.

—Jean Anouilh

只要你喜欢，事物就是美好的。

——让·阿努伊（法国剧作家）

It's not how much we give but how much love we put into giving.

—Mother Teresa

重要的不是我们给予了多少，而是我们在给予时投入了多少爱。

——特蕾莎修女

Those who are happiest are those who do the most for others.

—Booker T Washington

最快乐的人就是那些为别人做得最多的人。

——布克·华盛顿（美国政治家、教育家和作家）

There is nothing either good or bad but thinking makes it so.

—William Shakepeare

世界上的事情，无所谓好坏，关键在于怎么看。

——莎士比亚

There are lots of people I admire and respect, but I don't necessarily want to be like them. I'm too happy being myself.

—James Darcy

我欣赏和尊敬很多人，但这不代表我想变得和他们一样。做我自己就已经够快乐了。

——詹姆斯·达西（英国电影演员）绘英语

第2章

我不是胖，只是灵魂比较大

What Is the Meaning of Fat People's Life

(文© Claire J.Vannette)

I think we need fat people in this world so that those who are't fat can look at us and feel better about themselves. It's weird how that works but it's the truth. If you want to feel better about yourself, compare yourself to those who are less fortunate. What I want to know is what motivates us to keep living besides making people feel better.

Why wouldn't the usual reasons for living apply?

Goals and dreams. Loved ones. Pleasure and happiness. Curiosity. Religion and spirituality.

Being alive is pretty great. Sometimes, people decide it's not great, and in fact it's so terrible that they don't want to be alive anymore. But most of us try to keep living. Fat has nothing to do with that. Why would it? Maybe you think fat people are worthless. That says more about you than it does about fat people.

I imagine that what motivates them to keep living is their thoughts, ideas, feelings, passions, projects, goals, dreams. They live because they love, hate, cherish, yearn, despise and embrace.

What motivates them to keep living is who they are, not how they look.

圆滚滚的人生意义

（文◎克莱尔·J.瓦内特）

这个世界需要胖子，因为不胖的人只要瞅瞅我们就能获得不少心理慰藉。虽然挺浑蛋的，但事实就是这个理儿：我们总是通过旁人的不幸来证明自己的幸福。可我想知道，除了充当“心理安慰”，胖子们活着到底还有什么意义呢？

为什么就不能是出于简单寻常的理由呢？

目标和梦想，深爱的人们，纯粹的快乐，对未知的好奇，宗教信仰或者精神本质。

活着原本就是很伟大的事情，可有时候人们并不尊重生命的伟大，更可怕的是他们甚至不想活了。当然我们中大部分人都在努力地活下去，胖不胖与此毫无干系，难道不是吗？可能你会觉得胖子的人生就是一文不值的吧，我倒是觉得这个词用来形容你更为合适。

我想，是他们的思想、智慧、感受、热情、计划、目标、梦想激励着他们努力生活。他们活着，因为他们爱着、恨着、珍惜着、渴望着、憎恶着，也拥抱着。

他们活着，基于他们是谁，而不是他们长着一副什么模样。绘英语

The Most Beautiful Girl I Had Ever Met

(文◎ Chong Sheau Ching)

"Hi! How are you?" The woman smiled as she took the seat beside me. She had to lower herself slowly,squeezing her ample bottom into the seat, filling all available space. Positioning herself comfortably, she plopped her enormous arm on our common armrest. Her immensity saturated the space around us, shrinking me and my seat into insignificance.

I cringed and reclined towards the window. She repeated her greeting in an upbeat, friendly voice. "Hi." I replied with obvious loathing. I turned away to stare out the window, sulking silently about the long hours of discomfort I was going to experience with this monster beside me.

She nudged me with her meaty arm. "My name is Laura. I'm from Britain. ""Come on, if we're going to spend six hours side-by-side on this flight, we'd better be friends, don't you think?" I reluctantly stayed silent, but Laura took no notice of my unfriendly reactions. Instead, she started talking excitedly about herself and rattled on about her friends waiting for her now at our mutual destination; Indonesia.

I only gave one-word answers to her questions about me. Unperturbed by my coldness, she nodded as she made appreciative comments to them. She was particularly considerate and obliging when we were served drinks and meals, making sure that I had room to manoeuvre in my seat. "I don't want to clobber you with my elephant size!"she said with utmost sincerity.

After an hour or so, I couldn't help but let down my guard slowly. As much as she had repulsed me in

the beginning, she was an interesting conversationalist. She was well-read in many subjects, from philosophy to science. Her comments were humorous and inspirational.

"Have you ever thought about losing some weight?" I finally dared to ask after a while. "No. I've worked hard to get this way. Why would I want to give it up?" "You aren't worried about cardiovascular diseases that come with being overweight?"

"Not at all. You only get the diseases if you're worried about your weight all the time, but there is more in life than worrying about your weight. You always see advertisements from slimming centres that say: 'Liberate yourself from your extra baggage so that you are free to be yourself.' It's rubbish! You're liberated only if you're comfortable with who you are as a person and what you do. Why would I want to waste my time on slimming regimes when I have so many other important things to do and so many people to be friends with?"

"Folks often see me as a fat lady with big bosoms, big thighs and a big bottom. They see me as a slob. They think I'm lazy and have no willpower. They're wrong. I eat healthily and walk regularly, and I'm actually a slim person on the inside. I'm just so full of energy that people won't be able to keep up with me if I wasn't this size."

Our enthralling conversations had turned my flight into something thoroughly enjoyable. At the arrival lounge of Indonesia Capital Airport, we said goodbye. I watched her walking towards a big group of adoring adults and kids. Cheers sounded. Then, she turned around and winked at me. I was stunned, as the realisation set in: Laura was the most beautiful woman I had ever met in my life.

我见过的最漂亮的女孩

（文◎宗筱清）

“嗨，你好！” 这个女士一边坐在我旁边一边微笑着说。她必须慢慢地沉下身去，将她宽大的臀部挤入座位中，填满可用的空间。她坐舒坦之后，把她的粗大的胳膊“扑通”一声落在我们共用的扶手上。她的宽大体形渗透到我们周围的空间，也使我和我的座位缩小到可以无视的状态。

我畏缩地靠向窗子。她用愉快的声音又问候了一遍。 “嗨。”我以明显的厌恶的口气回答道。然后我转过头凝望着窗外，为将要和我旁边这个怪兽度过一段漫长时间的折磨人的旅程而生着闷气。

她用她肉肉的胳膊肘推了推我。“我名叫罗拉，来自英国。” “来嘛，如果我们将在这个航班上一起度过六个小时的话，我们最好能成为朋友，你觉得呢？”我很勉强地保持着沉默，但是罗拉对我不友好的反应毫不在意。反而，她开始很兴奋地谈关于她自己的事，而且喋喋不休地说她的朋友正在我们共同的目的地印度尼西亚等候她。

我对她的关于我的问题只用一个单词回答。她对我的冷漠泰然自若，一边对我的回答做出赞赏的表态一边点头。当送上餐饮服务时她表现得尤其体贴和有礼貌，确保我在座位上有活动的空间。“我不想用我大象般的体形使你为难！”她说的时候带着极大的真诚。

大约过了一个小时，我忍不住慢慢放松了我的戒备之心。就像她一开始用体形击溃了我一样，她也是一个很有趣的聊天伙伴。她在很多科目上都有所涉猎，从哲

学到科学。她的观点也幽默且鼓舞人心。

“你想过减减体重吗？”过了一会儿我终于斗胆问了她。“不。我费很大劲儿才到这种程度。我为什么要放弃呢？”“你就不担心伴随肥胖而来的心血管疾病吗？”

“完全不用。如果你总是担心你的体重你才会得这种病，但是生活中有比担心自己的体重更多的东西。你们总是从瘦身中心看到这样的广告：把你自己从额外的包袱中解放出来，你才能自由地做自己。这简直是胡说！只有当你为自己的生活方式和所作所为感到舒服的时候，自己才会真正地被解放。为什么我得在我有很多其他重要事情做的时候，有很多朋友可以结交的时候去浪费时间在瘦身养生的事情上？

“人们常将我看作一个有大胸脯、大粗腿和大屁股的胖女人。他们把我看作懒人。他们认为我懒惰且没有意志力。但他们错了。我饮食健康且经常散步，其实我内心里是一个很苗条的人。我就是浑身充满能量，如果我不是这种体形的话一般人不会追得上我。”

我们这段愉快的聊天使我的飞行变得十分开心。在印度尼西亚首都机场的抵达大厅，我们相互道别。我看着她走向一大群敬慕她的大人和孩子，他们欢呼雀跃。然后，她转过身并向我眨了眨眼睛。我被震惊了，这才意识到：罗拉是我生命中见过的最美丽的女士。

The F Word

(文◎ Anonymous)

"OK," I said to my daughter as she bent over her bowl of rice. "What's going on with you and J. ?""She's bossy," Lucy complained. "She's turning everyone against me."

Lucy muttered. "She's mean, she's bad at math, she's terrible at kickball and ... she's fat." "Excuse me," I said, struggling for calm. "What did you just say?" "She is fat," Lucy mumbled into her bowl. "We are going upstairs," I said, my voice cold.

I'd spent the nine years since her birth getting ready for this day, the day we'd have to have the conversation about this dreaded, stinging word. I knew exactly what to say to the girl on the receiving end of the taunts and the teasing, but in all of my imaginings, it never once occurred to me that my daughter would be the one who used the F word. Fat.

I am six years old, in first grade, and my father is hoisting—that's really the only word for it—me up into the backseat of the family's Chevy Suburban. "She's solid. She weighs 65 pounds," he's telling a friend. I am eight years old, sturdy bare legs dangling at the end of the examination table while my pediatrician, a woman with a soothing voice, and disconcertingly cool hands, tells my mom to stop packing me two sandwiches for lunch. And my mother, overweight herself, nods and says nothing.

How can anyone say no to food? I'm beginning to recognize that there are people born with an "off" switch, people to whom food, even the most delicious, is simply fuel. Then there are people like me, who eat every bite and still want more. I have no off switch. Happy, sad, lonely, content—the one constant in my life is hunger.

I'm 15, five-foot-six, 145 pounds. My parents have shipped me off on a teen tour to Israel. The group is filled with mean girls. There are five girls named Jennifer with my group that summer. "Oh, not the fat Jennifer," I hear one of my tour mates saying matter-of-factly to another.

I am incandescent with shame, knowing that fat is, by far, the worst thing you can be. Fat is lazy, fat is gross, fat is sloppy ... and, worst of all, fat is forever. I am fat—and, hence, undesirable, unlovable, a walking joke—for the rest of my life.

Then I'm 18, sitting in the dining hall across from the crew coach. I'd been a good rower in high school, good enough for Princeton to recruit me, but now I've gained the 15 pounds—one of my many bulimic freshmen classmates should have gained but didn't. "If you want to stay on the team," the coach tells me gently, "you're going to have to lose a lot of weight."

The coach relegates me to the worst boat and never makes eye contact with me again. The next year, I quit the team and join the school newspaper. I find my place, my calling. On the page, nobody can tell that you're fat.

I am 33, and after two days of labor followed by an emergency C-section, the doctor places my newborn daughter in my arms. At eight pounds, 11 ounces, she's one of the biggest babies in the nursery. I'm far too embarrassed to ask my doctor the only thing I want to know: Will she be normal, or will she be like me?

Now, at 42, I've made as much peace as a plus-size woman can make with her body. In my career, my weight has never held me back. I've worked for national newspapers, written best-selling novels, had a book turned into a movie, co-written a TV show that made it on the air. I have a job I love, two smart, funny daughters, a rich, full life with wonderful friends and a man who loves me ... but I know that, when the world sees me, they don't see any of this. They see fat.

My daughter sat on her bed, and I sat beside her. "How would you feel if someone made fun of you for something that wasn't your fault?" I began. "She could stop eating so much," Lucy mumbled, unwittingly mouthing the simple advice a thousand doctors and well-meaning friends and relatives have given overweight women for years.

"It's not always that easy," I said. "Everyone's different in terms of how they treat food." Do I tell her I didn't cry when someone posted my picture and commented underneath it, "I'm sorry, but aren't chick-lit authors supposed to be pretty?"

Words are my tools. Stories are my job. And I have no idea what to say. So I say to my daughter, "I love you, and there is nothing you could ever do to make me not love you. But I'm disappointed in you right now. There are plenty of reasons for not liking someone. What she looks like isn't one of them."

Lucy nods, tears on her cheeks. "I won't say that again," she tells me, and I pull her close, pressing my nose against her hair. So as we sit there together, I pray for her to be smart. I pray for her to be strong. I pray for her to find friends, work she loves, a partner who adores her, for her life to be easy, and for her to have the strength to handle it when it's not. And still, always, I pray that she will never struggle as I've struggled, that weight will never be her burden to bear.

“胖”这个字呀

（文◎佚名）

“好吧，”我对正在低头吃米饭的女儿说，“你和 J. 怎么了？”“她很横。”露西抱怨说，“她害得每个同学都针对我。”

她嘟囔着。“她很自私，数学不好，足球踢得很烂，而且……她很胖。”“等下，”我强作镇静，“你刚才说什么？”“她很胖。”露西一边吃饭一边含糊地说。“跟我上楼。”我冷冷地说。

终于得和女儿聊聊这个让人害怕、听着刺耳的字眼了，从她出生到今天，我已经准备了九年。对于遭受这种嘲讽和戏弄的女孩，我百分之百清楚该说些什么，但是我怎么也没想到，我自己的女儿正是那个说 F 词（胖）的人。

我 6 岁上小学一年级的时候，一次父亲把我抬（真的只有“抬”这个字最合适）到我家雪佛兰萨博班汽车的后座上，并对他的朋友说：“她长得很结实，有 65 磅（约 29.5 千克）重。”8 岁时，我坐在体检台的一头，晃悠着粗壮的光腿，听到我的儿科医生——一位声音轻柔、双手冰凉得令人不安的女士——告诉我母亲，午饭便当别给我带两个三明治了，太多了。而我那本身体重就超重的母亲点了点头，什么也没说。

谁又能对吃的说不呢？我渐渐明白，有的人生来嘴上就有道“闸”，食物，哪怕是最美味的食物对他们来说也不过是给身体提供能量的东西；可也有人像我一样，吃得再多也不够。我嘴上没有那道“闸”。无论是高兴还是伤心，孤单还是满足，我的人生一直处于饥饿的状态。

15 岁时，我已经有 5 英尺 6 英寸（约 167.6 厘米）高，145 磅（约 65.8 千克）重了。父母把我送去参加一个赴以色列的青少年游学团，这个团里有很多刻薄的女孩。那年夏天，我所在的小组有五个叫珍妮弗的女孩。“哦，不是那个胖珍妮弗。”我听到一个团员直言不讳地跟另一个这么说。

我羞愤难当，觉得肥胖是到那时为止我人生中最糟糕的事。肥胖意味着懒惰，意味着恶心，意味着邋遢……最糟糕的是，肥胖会永远伴随着我。我胖，所以我不受人欢迎，不招人待见，走到哪儿都被人笑话，余生都会这样。

18 岁那年，我在食堂吃饭，对面坐着划艇队的教练。我在高中时就已是一名出色的桨手了，因表现出众被普林斯顿大学录取。但如今，我体重增加了 15 磅（约 6.8 千克），我那些患有贪食症的大一同班新生本该变胖却也长不了这么多肉。“你如果想继续待在队里，”教练温和地说，“就必须减掉很多体重。”

教练把我“调”到最差的一艘划艇上，然后再也没和我有过眼神交流。一年后，我退出了划艇队，加入了校报。我找准了自己的位置，找到了我的职业方向。在报纸上，没人能看出来你是不是胖子。

33 岁时，经历了两天的分娩和随后的紧急剖宫产，医生让我抱上了刚刚出生的女儿。她有 8 磅 11 盎司（约 4 千克）重，是育儿室里最重的婴儿之一。我太过难为情，都没有问医生我唯一想问的那个问题：她会是个正常人还是会像我一样胖？

如今，42 岁的我已经做到尽可能平和地看待自己大一号的身体。我的体重从来没有阻碍我的职业发展。我为几家全国性的报刊供稿，写了许多畅销小说，有一本书已被改编为电影，而且与别人合写了一部电视剧并成功播出。我有一份自己热爱的工作，有两个聪明有趣的女儿，生活充实富足，有许多非常棒的朋友，还有一个爱我的男人……但我知道，世人在看到我时，看不到这一切，他们只会看到我很胖。

露西坐在她的床上，我坐在她旁边。“如果有人取笑你，但取笑你的原因并不是你的错，你会怎么想？”我开始发话了。“她可以少吃点儿。”露西含糊地回答。她不经意间说出的这句话正是多年来医生们和好心的亲朋好友都会给肥胖女性的简单建议。

“这件事并不总是那么容易，”我说，“每个人对待食物的态度各不相同。”曾经有人贴出我的照片并在下面评论说：“借问一句，小妞文学的作者难道不该是美女吗？”我要不要告诉女儿，我当时并没因此而哭泣？

语言是我的工具，讲故事是我的工作，而我现在却不知道该说些什么。于是我对女儿说：“我爱你，无论你做什么我都不会不爱你。但是我现在对你很失望。不喜欢一个人可以有许多原因，但外表一定不是其中一个。”

露西点点头，脸上还挂着泪花。“我不会再说那样的话了。”她对我说。我把她揽了过来，鼻子贴着她的头发。我们一起坐在那里，我祈祷她将来成为一个聪明、坚强的女孩；祈祷她能交到朋友，找到喜欢的工作，拥有爱她的伴侣；祈祷她的人生旅途一帆风顺，祈祷她在遇到坎坷时也能够有力量去处理。而且，如以往一般，我祈祷她永远不会像我曾经那般挣扎，祈祷她的体重永远不会成为她背上的重担。

I'm a Fat Admirer
Who Lost Weight

(文◎KC Morley)

In the past few years, I've come out as a female fat admirer in my online and real life interactions. I have loudly and proudly acknowledged my unabashed attraction to bigger body types, both male and female. I have spoken to friends, acquaintances and even total strangers, and found out that there are women out there like me—and many men as well—who appreciate a fuller body. Personally, I love a man with a beer belly or a woman with a whole lot of booty. I like big arms and chubby cheeks.

I'm attracted to fat people. And I've gone from being quiet about it to being very vocal, from stating my preferences without hesitation to correcting language and attitudes that are harmful and hurtful.

I've also gone from a size 14 to a size 6.

I'd like to say it was for health reasons. That it was an unintended side effect of living in one of the healthiest and most active states in the nation. That it was because of my health problems, or the medications I take. But that would be a lie.

I do like to rationalize it by pointing out that I'm really quite short with a very small bone structure, so a size 14 on me compared to a size 14 on someone 6 inches taller is really quite a profound difference.

But that's just an excuse.

The fact is, I made a conscious decision to lose weight

through dieting and working with personal trainers over a period of several years because, as a fat girl, I was miserable.

Believe me, I am hanging my head in shame as I write this. I—the fat admirer who preaches about accepting your body the way it is, being proud—used to cry myself to sleep at night because I hated myself so much. In fact, I destroyed every photograph of the years I was at my heaviest. There is no visual evidence of me in my early 20s. I have eradicated that fat self entirely.

I have long meditated on what causes the disconnect between what I like on myself and what I like on others. Quite frankly, it makes no sense. I've never had an "Ew, gross!" reaction to fat people. Usually, I'm intrigued. It catches my eyes. It makes me want to keep looking. It makes me want to touch. I enjoy the contours. So I've analyzed, and contemplated, and thought, and processed. And I've worried—am I merely fetishizing? Exoticizing something that is different from myself in an attempt to abate my fear of it?

So what else could it be? Many people who have been fat can probably relate to this: Despite being a size 6 now, I still feel like a fat girl. When I hear anyone speaking in a derogatory manner about fat people, I always feel as though they're talking about me. I take that sort of commentary very personally. And any time I hear anyone talk about struggles with weight and body image, I know exactly what they're feeling. Our culture's unrealistic beauty standards make me cringe. The fashion industry pisses me off on a regular basis. The fact that there are people in the world who think that fat is gross makes my blood boil. I recently shocked a muscular male co-worker who was speaking negatively about "fat chicks" by informing him that there are those in the world, myself included, who don't find his body or bodies like his attractive. I assure you all, the look on his face was priceless.

I keep telling myself, and anyone else willing to listen, that the difference between that co-worker and me is that I would never look at a body builder and say, "Ew, gross!" I would never look at a muscular person and say they're disgusting, or that there is something wrong with them, or that they're unattractive. I would look at a muscular body and admire the amount of work and dedication it takes to achieve and maintain that sort of physique. Maybe it's not my thing, but it's still beautiful.

But all the good and healthy attitudes and commentaries I participate in and encourage in others don't erase this bothersome little hypocrisy of mine. I have to admit, with much sadness, that somewhere inside of this complicated mess of a psyche, I have a problem with fat.

And there it is. Yes, I confess, I watch my scale obsessively and track my calories on a neat little iPhone app and continue to work with a personal trainer and read the ingredients and nutritional information on every food product I buy and change my clothes five times every morning until I find an outfit that makes me feel skinny and suffer from crippling guilt when I skip the gym. Because I, ladies and gentleman, seem to have a problem with fat.

At least, I have a problem with fat on me. But on the rest of you, I think it's sexy as hell.

心里藏着胖子的瘦姑娘

（文◎ KC. 莫莉 译◎ 张玲）

在过去几年里，无论是在网上还是在现实生活中，我总是宣称自己是一个喜欢胖的女孩。我曾大声并骄傲地承认：丰腴的体形对我有着无法掩饰的吸引力，不论是男性还是女性。我和朋友、熟人甚至是完全陌生的人都谈论过这个话题，结果发现确实有女性——也有许多男性——像我一样喜欢更丰满的身材。从我个人来说，我喜欢腆着啤酒肚的男人或者是臀部浑圆的女人。我喜欢粗壮的胳膊和胖嘟嘟的脸蛋。

胖子对我很有吸引力。以前我不敢在人前坦言这一点，现在却对此直言不讳。开始我只是毫不犹豫地阐明自己在这方面的喜好，现在我只要听到有损或伤害胖子的言论，就会出言纠正。

而我的衣服尺码却也从 14 码缩水到了 6 码。

我想说这是出于对健康的考虑，这是因生活在美国最健康、最有活力的州而收获的并非出于我本意的意外效果，这是由于我的健康问题或者是我服用药物的结果。但这些都是谎话。

我的确很想为“变瘦”找个合理的解释，比如说我个子很矮，骨架很小，所以一件 14 码的衣服穿在比我高 6 英寸（约 15.2 厘米）的人身上与穿在我身上，看起来那真是天壤之别。

但这纯属借口。

事实是，在长达若干年的时间里，我一直在通过节食并跟着私人教练健身来减肥，减肥是我做出的清醒的决定。因为身为一个胖女孩，我感到很痛苦。

相信我，我写下这段话时正羞愧地低着头。我——一个到处鼓吹接受你现在的身材并为之感到骄傲的肥胖爱好者——过去常常在夜晚伴着泪水入眠，因为我恨极了自己。实际上，我把自己在最胖那几年拍的所有照片都销毁了。我没有给 20 岁出头时的自己留下任何看得到的视觉资料。我已经将那个胖姑娘彻底从我的生命中剔除了。

我希望自己成为一个样儿，又希望别人成为另一个样儿，是什么原因使我产生了这种割裂的想法呢？长时间以来我一直在思考这个问题。很坦白地说，这种想法没有任何意义。对于胖子，我从未有过“噢，丑死了”的反应。通常情况下，我都会被吸引。胖子会抓住我的眼球，让我想一直看个够，还忍不住想摸一摸。我喜欢那种身段。所以，我已分析过，琢磨过，思考过，想过这是为什么。我也担心过——我是不是纯属盲目迷恋？还是有意把与自己不同的事物“异域和迷人化”，以试图减轻自己对它的恐惧心理？

还能有什么其他的解释吗？许多曾经胖过的人可能会理解这种情形：尽管我现在穿6码的衣服，我还是感觉自己很胖。只要听到有人用贬损的口吻谈论胖人，我总觉得他们好像是在议论我。我以为那些话是专门针对我的。不管什么时候我听到有人谈论他们跟体重、身材做斗争的经历，我都完全理解他们的感受。我们文化中对美的不现实的评判标准令我畏缩。时尚产业则经常让我气不打一处来。这个世界上还有人认为肥胖是令人恶心的，这一事实令我怒火中烧。不久前我就着实让一个“肌肉男”同事震惊了一回：他当时正在出言不逊地谈论“胖妞”话题，我就告诉他这个世界上还有些人——包括我在内——丝毫不觉得他的身材或者像他那样的身材有什么吸引力。我向你们保证，他脸上的表情滑稽极了。

我不断地告诉自己和其他所有愿意听我倾诉的人，我的那个同事和我之间最大的区别在于，我永远不会看着一个健美运动员对他说：“噢，太丑了！”我永远不会对着一个肌肉发达的人说他们让我感到恶心，或者说他们有这样那样的问题，或者说他们不够吸引人。看见健美的身材，我会钦佩人们为练出并保持那样的体形而付出的辛苦和努力。或许那不是我的“菜”，但它依然很美。

然而，尽管我行事时态度端正、言辞健康，并鼓励别人也这么做，但还是无法消除我内心那令人讨厌的小小伪善。我必须悲哀地承认，在这个复杂、混乱的心灵的某个地方，我有一个关于肥胖的心结。

它就在那里。是的，我坦白，我会着了迷一样地盯着体重秤上的指针；我用苹果手机上的一款简洁的小应用软件记录我摄入的卡路里数量；我继续跟着私人教练健身；我阅读自己买的每一种食品包装上的成分和营养信息；我每天早晨换五套衣服，直到找到一套让自己觉得显瘦的；我要是翘课没去健身就会深感内疚，饱受煎熬。因为，各位女士、先生，我似乎有一个关于肥胖的心结。

至少，我这个心结是针对长在我自己身上的肥肉。但如果这些肥肉长在你们身上，我觉得那非常性感！

If We Give up Body Shame, the World Will Be Beautiful

（文◎ Jordyn Taylor）

Who knew there were so many ways to body shame women using seemingly innocuous office supplies?

Now there's a new social media challenge designed to make women feel bad about their bodies. Spawned from the social media site Weibo, the so-called "A4 Waist Challenge" has women comparing the width of their waists tothe short side of a sheet of printer paper, and sadly, it's going viral.

The challenge, which inherently equates success with having a small waist size, has become a trending topic on Weibo, garnering more than 40,000 commenters and people sharing their own challenge photos.

Despite the challenge's popularity, here's why not to get caught up in it. In 2012, the average U.S. woman's waist size was 37.8 inches. The short side of an A4 sheet of paper measures 8.3 inches — less than a quarter of the average American woman's waist. Hiding your waist behind an A4 sheet of paper isn't something everyone — or even the average U.S. woman — is able to do.

That being said, whether you're able to do it isn't even important. Some waists are wide and some waists are narrow — it's true. But neither should be automatically associated with ugliness or failure. Forget fat shaming and skinny shaming — all waist sizes are gorgeous, people.

如果人人都放弃身材羞辱，这世界将变成美好人间

（文◎乔丁·泰勒 译◎小J）

谁能想到，可以用那么多种看起来无伤大雅的办公用品对女性进行身材羞辱？

现在社交网络上又有了一种新挑战，其设计就是为了让女人觉得自己的身材糟透了。名为“挑战A4腰”的活动在微博发酵，要求女人用一张打印纸的宽度来衡量自己的腰围。令人无语的是，这种挑战像病毒一样火速蹿红。

这种本质上将成功和细腰画等号的挑战成为微博上的热门话题，获得了四万条评论，人们纷纷上传自己的照片参加挑战。

尽管这种挑战大热，我们也不应该跟风。2012年，美国女性的平均腰围是37.8英寸（约96厘米）。A4纸的宽为8.3英寸（约21厘米）——比美国女性平均腰围的四分之一还要细。把你的腰藏在一张A4纸后面不是随便谁就能做到的，一般的美国女性都做不到。

这就是说，你能不能做到压根儿不重要。有的人腰粗有的人腰细，这是事实。但是这些都不该与丑陋或失败自动联系起来。忘记肥胖羞辱或瘦子羞辱吧——每种腰围都是美的。

I Am Pretty, I Am Foodie

（文◎ Anonymous）

Some people say that business about the jolly fat person is a myth, that all of us chubbies are neurotic, sick, sad people. I disagree . Fat people may not be chortling all day long, but they're a hell of a lot nicer than the wizened and shriveled. Thin people turn surly, mean, and hard at a young age because they never learn the value of a hot–fudge sundae for easing tension. Thin peole don't like gooey soft things because they themselves are neither gooey nor soft. They are crunchy and dull, like carrots. They go straight to the heart of the matter while fat people let things stay all blurry and hazy and vague, the way things actually are. Thin people want to face the truth. Fat people know there is no truth. One of my thin friends always staring at the complex , unsolvable problems and saying, "the key thing is..."Fat people never say that. They know there isn't any such thing as the key thing about anything.

Thin people believe in logic. Fat people see all sides. The sides fat people see are rounded blobs, usually gray, always nobulous and truly not worth worrying about. But the thin person persists."if you coonsume more calories than your burn. you will gain weight. It's that simple. "Fat people always grin when

they hear statements like that. They know better.

Fat people realize that life is a illogical and unfair. They know very well that God is not in his heaven and all is not right with the world. If God was up there, fat people could have two doughnuts and a big orange drink anytime they wanted it.

Thin people have a long list of logical things they are always spouting off to me. They hold up one finger at a time as they reel off these things, so I won't lose track. They speak slowly as if to a young child. The list is long and fool of holes. It contains tidbits like"get a grip on yourself, ""cigarettes kill, ""cholesterol clogs, ""fit as fiddle, ""ducks in a row, ""organize, "and "sound fiscal management." Phrases like that.

They think these 2,000-point plans lead to happiness. Fat people know happiness is elusive at best and even if they could get the kind think people talk about, they wouldn't want it. Wisely, fat people see that such programs are too dull, too hard, too off the mark. They are never better than a whole cheese cake.

Fat people know all about mystery of life. They are the ones acquainted with the night, with luck, with fat, with playing it by ear. One thin person I know once suggested that we arrange all the parts of a jigsaw puzzle into groups according to size, shape, and color. He figured this would but the time needed to complete the puzzle by at least 50 percent. I said I wouldn't do it. One, I like to muddle through. Two, what good would it do to finish

early? Three, the jigsaw puzzle isn't the important thing. The important thing is the fun of four people (one thin person included) sitting around a card table , working on a jigsaw puzzle.

The main problem with thin people is they oppress. Their good intentions, bony torsos, tight ships, neat corners, cerebral machinatins, and pat solutions loom like dark clouds over the loose, comfortable, spread-out, soft wortd of the fat. Long after fat people have removed their coats and shoes and put their feet up on the coffee table, thin people are still sitting on the edge of the sofa, looking neat as a pin, discussing rutabagas. Fat people are heavily into fits of laughter, slapping their thighs and whooping it up, while thin people are still politely waiting for the punch line.

Thin people are downers. They like math and morality and reasoned uation of the limitations of human beings. They have their skinny little acts together. They expound, prognose, probe.

Fat people are convivial. They will like you even if you're irregular and have acne. They will come up with a good reason why you never wrote the great American novel. They will cry in your beer with you. They will put your name in the pot. They will let you off the hook. Fat people will gab, giggle, guffaw, gallumph, and gossip. They are generous, giving, and gallant. They are glutonous and goodly and great. What you want when you're down is soft and jiggly, not muscled and stable. Fat people know this. Fat people have plenty of room. Fat people will take you in.

我很好看，也很好吃

（文◎佚名）

有人觉得我们活泼开朗的胖子不可理喻。像我们长着胖胖的脸蛋的人就应该神经兮兮，病恹恹，多愁善感。我不同意这种说法。胖子未必一整天都是乐呵呵的，尽管这样他们也比那些干瘪的瘦子活得开心得多。瘦子年纪轻轻就养成了一副坏脾气，变得苛刻，顽固。这是因为他们不知道吃个圣代冰淇淋对缓解压力有多大的帮助。瘦子不爱甜软的食物，因为他们自己长得又干又硬，更别说甜美可爱了。他们既脆弱又无味，就像萝卜。他们一针见血，而胖子则喜欢稀里糊涂，顺其自然，按部就班。瘦子总是在挖掘真理，而胖子明白世上根本就不存在真理。我的一个瘦子朋友总是在解决那些错综复杂的棘手难题，还说道：“关键在于……”胖子从不那么说，因为任何事情都没有关键所在。

瘦子相信逻辑，胖子看问题面面俱到。胖子看到的往往是模糊朦胧的一团乱麻，根本就没什么值得担心的。瘦子却在坚持：“如果你吸收的热量超过你消耗的热量，你就会变得更胖。”听了这些话，

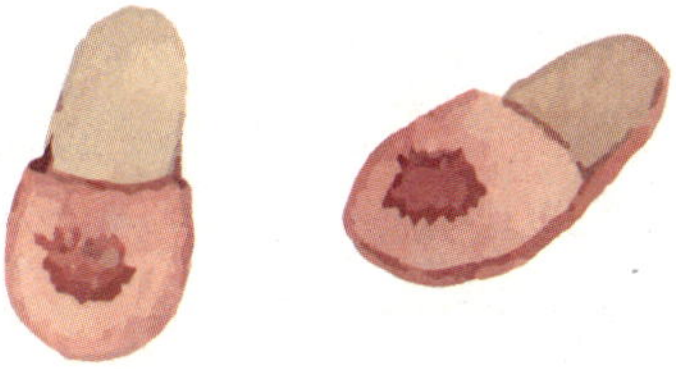

胖子总会咧嘴一笑，其实对此他们比谁都明白。

胖子意识到生活既无逻辑也不公平。上帝根本就不存在，更不会主持公道。如果真有上帝的话，那么上帝就能随时在他们想吃两个炸面圈和喝一大杯橙汁的时候满足他们的愿望。

瘦子总在对我滔滔不绝地讲一连串有逻辑的事情。他们每讲完一件，就伸一根手指记着，我就没法走神了。他们慢吞吞地讲话，好像把我当孩子一样。他们讲得那么多，而且漏洞百出。其中经常出现这些词句，比如“把握自己”“吸烟有害健康”“胆固醇阻塞”“体壮如牛”“计划组织”“合理管理财政”。

他们认为这份包括 2000 个要点的计划意味着幸福快乐。胖子却懂得幸福是难以捉摸的，就算他们具备了瘦子列出的所有条件，他们也不会稀罕。他们太明智了，看得清这种计划太无聊，太艰苦，太不实际。还不如一个奶酪蛋糕来得现实些。

胖子理解生活的痛苦。他们珍惜夜晚的时光、好运气和自己的命运，不管明天怎样只管享受眼前。我认识一个瘦子，他建议我们在玩拼图的时候，按照形状、大小和颜色来拼，这样可以节省一半的时间。我可不愿那么干。第一，我喜欢稀里糊涂地做事情。第二，早早结束游戏有什么好处？第三，拼图本身并不重要，要紧的是享受四个人（包括那个瘦子）围着一张牌桌玩拼图的乐趣。

瘦子最大的问题在于他们使人感到压抑。他们的野心勃勃、瘦骨嶙峋的身体、高速的节拍、干净利落的屋角、大脑的机械运作方式和当机立断像乌云一样笼罩着胖子那松弛、舒适、广阔、温馨的世界。胖子早已脱掉外套和鞋子，把脚翘到咖啡桌上的时候，瘦子却还一本正经地坐在沙发上，木头钉似的直挺着脊背谈论着丑女人。当胖子哈哈大笑，拍着大腿兴奋地欢呼时，瘦子却还在恭恭敬敬地寻找着关键词语。

瘦子沉闷压抑。他们热爱数学、道德规范和对人类劣根性的理性评价。他们行为琐碎繁多，好辩论，好预测未来，好追根究底。

胖子爱交际。就算你喜怒无常，或脸上长满痘子，他们还是一样地喜欢你。他们会给你一个理由，解释你为什么写不出美国最好看的小说。他们会与你一起借酒消愁。他们会把你放在心上，他们会帮你摆脱困境。胖子絮叨，傻笑，开怀大笑，打打闹闹，还好说闲话。但他们慷慨，宽容，讲义气。他们贪吃，爱臭美，简直是完美的。胖子懂得人伤心的时候需要好言相劝，而不是泼冷水以及硬邦邦的敷衍。胖子心宽体胖，一定能容得下你。

Free to Be Fat

(文◎ David Haslam)

The classic 1981 horror movie *The Monster Club*, starring Vincent Price, Donald Pleasance, and John Carradine as monsters, included a cast of cannibals, vampires, werewolves, ghouls, and a hybrid creature called a "shadmock." Among this group of misfits, the only outcast was an ordinary fat girl.

Hollywood did not invent the concept of the fat-monster. In 1770, an English miller named Thomas Wood became the world's first weight-loss celebrity. Promoting "abstemious warfare", Wood was known as "Monster Miller." At 43, he suffered from obesity, along with arthritis, gout, indigestion, and "raging thirst" (possibly diabetes), as well as almost suicidal depression.

But Wood transformed himself "from a monster to a person of moderate size; from the condition of an unhealthy, decrepit, old man, to perfect health, and to the vigor and activity of youth" by following the diet regimen described in Luigi Cornaro's 1558 book *The Life of Cornaro.* Wood was highly regarded by his clients, visiting admirers' homes and regaling them with stories of fat people suffering ghastly deaths.

The obese were not always considered monsters. On the contrary, until recently they were often revered. Historically, in most societies, obesity implied wealth and health– expensive epicurean habits and no tuberculosis, cholera, or other wasting illnesses. Only now, when fat people outnumber the lean by two to one in many countries, has obesity become the last acceptable target of public discrimination.

Consider the Venus of Willendorf, a small statuette discovered inAustriain 1908 by archeologist Josef Szombathy. She has a huge abdomen, enormous breasts, and large buttocks, hips, and thighs. At around 25,000 years old, she was considered perhaps the world's oldest piece of figurative art, until September 2008, when archeologists discovered an even older piece– an ivory figurinefrom southwest Germany –estimated to be 35,000–40,000 years old. Remarkably, it, too, is a small statuette representing an obese woman: the Venus of Hohle Fels.

Much conjecture surrounds these discoveries. They are generally assumed to have been either fertility symbols or Mother Goddesses. One theory suggests that they were prehistoric equivalents of *Playboy* magazines Girl of the Month. Whatever their significance, they were evidently objects of reverence, not disdain.

Many great historical figures have suffered from obesity without discrimination. American President William Howard Taft and British Prime Minister Winston Churchill were obese, as was Britain's Queen Victoria. Great writers and artists–Henry James, Gioacchino Rossini, and Alfred Hitchcock, for example–carried their weight without public humiliation.

But, even in the fat–friendlier past, the overweight faced the harsh verdict of medical critics. In 1839, for example, British doctor J.G. Milligan wrote that the obese possess "indolence and apathy... laxity of fibre." In 1924, French physician Jean Frumusan described the "torpid" obese: "pale and puffy, whose flesh is swollen as if by liquids. Their emotivity is always exaggerated, and although cloaked by an apparent indifference, their exaggerated sensitivities make their lives a perpetual tragedy."

Nowadays, Western societies tend to blame the victim, especially when it comes to obese children

But the boy does not control his diet or exercise; his nutrition and activity are usually closely supervised. His obesity partly reflects his mother's lifestyle when he was in utero, and his family's lifestyle after he was born. He has had obesity thrust upon him, and with it a dysfunctional metabolism, chronic illness, and a shortened life. He already has enough problems without society ganging up on him for being a fatso.

Yet researchers have found that children as young as six years old, even those who are overweight themselves,use words like "lazy" "stupid " "cheats" "liars""sloppy" "naughty""mean" and "ugly"to describe their obese peers. Similarly, recent studies of college students show that respondents

rate obese individuals as less attractive potential partners than embezzlers, cocaine users, and shoplifters.

Obese people often share society's low opinion of them. Of one group whose members lost weight after surgery, 42% claimed that they would rather go blind than regain it. Most would rather lose a leg, and all would prefer deafness, dyslexia, diabetes, severe heart disease, or acne.

Even today,some doctors partake in the ubiquitous anti-obesity discrimination that feeds such sentiments. To be sure, most recognize that obesity is a multifactor chronic disease requiring medical, societal, environmental, and political interventions, But that enlightened approach did not stop Hamish Meldrum, Chairman of the British Medical Association (and one of Britain's most outspoken physicians), from recently offering this assessment of the obese: "They are just greedy."

Meldrum's remark reflects a widespread view of those who are overweight. But it is not the people maligned by such calumnious statements who are the monstrous ones.

胖的自由

（文◎大卫·哈斯拉姆 译◎开始）

1981 年的经典恐怖电影《怪物俱乐部》中，由文森特·普莱斯、唐纳德·普莱森斯和约翰·卡拉丁饰演怪物，包括食人生番、吸血鬼、狼人、食尸怪，以及一种叫 shadmock 的混血兽。在这群格格不入的家伙中，唯一的流浪者是个普通的胖女孩。

好莱坞的胖怪物概念并非空穴来风。1770 年，一位名唤托马斯·伍德的磨坊主成了世上首位减肥明星。伍德提倡“节食战争”，被称为“怪物磨坊主”。他 43 岁时患有肥胖症，伴有关节炎、痛风、消化不良，还有“难受的口渴”（也许是糖尿病），并且严重抑郁恨不得自杀。

但是伍德遵从路易吉·科尔纳罗 1558 年的作品《科尔纳罗的生活》中描述的养生饮食法，把自己“从怪物变成了身材适中的人，从病态、衰弱、年迈的身体状况变成青年般的生机勃勃”。伍德深受主顾们的尊敬，到处造访仰慕者的家，并与他们分享身材肥胖者恐怖死法的故事。

肥胖者并不总是被视为怪物。相反，直到最近，他们常常为人所敬仰。历史上在大多数时代里

肥胖意味着财富和健康——昂贵精致的生活习惯，没有肺结核、霍乱或者其他消耗性疾病。直至现在，当许多国家里胖子以 2 ： 1 的比例超过瘦子时，肥胖才成为最后一个为人津津乐道的大众歧视的靶子。

想想看，1908 年由考古学家约瑟夫・松鲍蒂发现的小雕像维伦多尔夫女神，她的肚子、胸部、屁股、腰围和大腿无一不肥硕有加。她大概有 25000 年的历史，被认为可能是世上最古老的具象艺术作品，直到 2008 年考古学家发现了一件更古老的——来自德国西南部的一尊象牙小雕像，据推测有 35000~40000 年的历史。引人注目的是，它也是一尊体现胖女性的小雕像：霍勒菲尔斯的维纳斯。

围绕这些发现产生了很多推测。一般认为她们要么是生殖繁衍的象征，要么是地母娘娘。有一个理论认为她们相当于《花花公子》杂志上的封面女郎。不管其意义究竟是什么，她们显然是崇仰而非鄙视的对象。

有很多伟大的历史巨人，身材肥胖却无人歧视。美国前总统威廉・霍华德・塔夫脱和英国前首相温斯顿・邱吉尔是胖子，英国维多利亚女王亦然。伟大的作家和艺术家们，比如亨利・詹姆斯、焦阿基诺・罗西尼和阿尔弗莱德・希区柯克——大腹便便却不曾受人白眼。

但是，即使是在对肥胖的态度较为友好的过去，肥胖者还是面临来自医学评论家们的尖刻指责。比如，1839 年英国医生 J.G. Milligan 写道，肥胖者“懒惰而冷漠……吃了纤维就腹泻”。1924 年法国医生 Jean Frumusan 这样描述“懒散的”肥胖者：“苍白而浮肿，肉体里仿佛注进了液体。往往多愁善感，尽管表面上无动于衷，但实际上过度的敏感使他们的人生成为永远的悲剧。”

今天西方社会倾向于指责受害者，尤其是在胖的是孩子的时候。

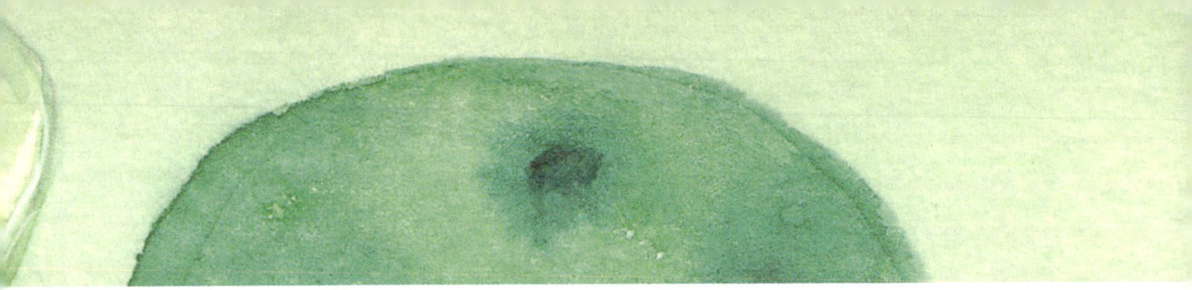

但是普通的男孩并不能控制自己的饮食或者运动；他的营养和活动都处在监控之下。他的肥胖症部分地反映了出生前他母亲的生活习惯和出生后他家庭的生活习惯。他的肥胖症是外界强加在他身上的，同样还有新陈代谢紊乱、慢性疾病，以及寿命缩短。在全社会因为他是个胖子就联起手来对付他之外，他已经有太多的麻烦了。

但是研究人员发现年仅6岁的儿童，即使自己也体重超标，都会使用“懒惰”“愚蠢”“作弊”“撒谎”“马虎”“淘气”“小气”和“丑陋”之类的词语来描述其他肥胖的同伴。同样，最近对大学生的研究显示，受访者把肥胖者视为比侵吞公款者、可卡因吸食者和商店小偷更可能不受欢迎的伙伴。

肥胖者往往承受了社会对他们的恶劣评价。有一群手术减肥成功的人，其中42% 的人声称他们宁愿瞎了眼也不愿再胖起来。他们当中大多数人宁愿断腿，所有的人宁愿耳聋，有阅读障碍，得糖尿病、严重的心脏病，或者长痤疮。

即使在今天，有些医生也加入了无处不在的反肥胖的歧视队伍，助长了这种情绪。诚然，大多数人认识到肥胖是一种多重因素引起的慢性疾病，需要医学的、社会的、环境的和政治的干预。但是这些再三强调的方法并没有阻止英国医学会主席Hamish Meldrum（英国最直言的医生之一）最近发表的对肥胖者的评论：“他们只是贪吃而已。”

Meldrum 的话反映了大多数人对肥胖者的看法。但是，真正的怪物并不是那些被此类污蔑言语中伤的人。

How to Express "You Become More Overweight" Gracefully
如何优雅地把"你胖了"说成一句情诗

（文◎ Anonymous 佚名）

The moment you enter my world,
I care for nothing but you.
你的出现吸引了我全部的视线。
Silently and motionlessly as we stand,
we get closer with time.
我们就这样默默站着不动，可距离又近了一厘米。
I cannot see anyone but you.
我的眼睛里全是你。
The longer we are together,
the fonder my heart becomes towards you.
你在我心中，分量越来越重。
Sweetheart, I delight at your satisfied stomach.
亲爱的最近很开心，胃口很好，我真高兴。
Holding her, I utter my wonder:
is it that my hands turned shorter?
搂着她对她说，我的手是变短了吗？
With every minute, I feel your weightiness.
你对我越来越重要。
Oh my silly,
see how you get chubby as the temperature increases?
傻瓜，你怎么随着温度的升高丰满了？
Perhaps it is time for us to renew your closet.
我再给你买几件新衣服吧！
Her hand in mine and under the moonshine,
she hears me sigh: soon, you will be as full as the moon.
月夜，牵起她的手说：月圆人更圆。
The day we part, thousand miles from each other we are,
you are still in my sight.
我送你离开，千里之外，你依然还在。

Stop Talking, Kiss Me
别说话，吻我

（文◎ Landy 兰迪）

我希望能有一
个好身材。
但我没那么想
节食。

我希望今年夏天能
给大家展现一副
好身材，但是有个
小问题……
我在乎大家的看法，
但我更在乎好吃的。

其实我身体里住着一
个瘦子
但是我一直往嘴里塞
饼干
挡住了她唯一的出路。

我费了那么大劲儿
爬到食物链顶端
不是为了吃素的。

大部分时间我都处
在失魂落魄的状态。
只有一件事能让我
专心致志，
又到吃饭的时间啦。

如果没人看见你
吃东西，
你就可以当作
没吃。

在食物这个问题上
没有“我们”，
都是“我”的。

胖了几斤真不是
什么大不了的事儿。
如果有人想绑架你，
他都得算计算计
绳子的成本。

我超爱我的六块腹肌，
为了保护它们
我特意在上面盖上
了一层肥肉。

我一直在甩肉，
但是肉一直在黏我。

我之所以吃蛋糕是
因为
世界那么大
肯定有人今天
过生日。

安静的女孩 Quiet Girl

I would liken you
To a night without star
Were it not for your eyes.

I would liken you
To a sleep without dreams
Were it not for your songs.

倘若不是因为你的眼睛，
我会把你比作
没有星星的夜晚。

倘若不是因为你的歌声，
我会把你比作
无梦的睡眠。

（文◎Langston 兰斯顿·休斯 译◎徐翰林）

第3章

写给食物的情书

Longing Is Another Form of Divine Instruction

（文◎ Anonymous）

Too often we deem our desires to be frivolous. Those of the ego we can live without. However, there is a knowing that resides much deeper. Needs of the soul require attention if you're to ever know peace.

欲望是另一种神祇

（文◎佚名）

我们往往认为自己的欲望是负面的东西，这些来自本我的情绪是我们可以克服的。然而，其实我们内心深谙另一个道理。那就是，来自心灵的欲望也需要得到自己的关注，只有这样你才能获得内心的平静。

Love Letter to Food

（文◎ Anonymous）

Dear Food, Dear Food, I know you already know this, but I need you, You bring my family together, you sweeten my celebrations, you make my deals, you satisfy my senses, and you keep me alive.

You work so hard to make all of this possible,spending your life growing in the field,the factory or the sea. I try to be good to you. I give you half of my land,two thirds of the water I consume,a tenth of my energy and one-sixth of my workforce. But I want to apologize. Because after all that, you deserve to be eaten. But instead,I throw away almost half of you enough calories to feed 150 million people.

From harvest to home, I waste half of all fruits, vegetables, seafood, and a third of all grains. I'm better to meat and dairy,wasting only 20 percent, but this is a double waste, because essentially I'm also dumping the grain or grass the animals ate to make the muscle or milk. And I waste you in many ways: For example, sometimes I leave you in the field to die because it costs more to harvest you than you're worth.

Other times, I mistakenly damage, contaminate, or spill you. Or, I reject you when you're imperfect, because I judge by appearance. But mostly I squander you in supermarkes, restaurants and homes, when you are so close to being eaten. I offer too much of you, so I take too much and I can't finish you, or I can't sell all of you before you go bad. At home I forget about you or I cook too much and don't know how to store you.

Or maybe I just don't like leftovers. Part of the problem is that on average, I spend a smaller fraction of my household budget on you than in any other country or any time in history, and my spending is spread out over days and weeks, so I don't notice the cost of wasting you. But my lack of noticing adds up: I devote four California's worth of land and more water than all non-agricultural water consumption combined just do grow food that doesn't get eaten.

This is not your fault—it's time. Only I can buy less of you and eat more of what I do buy. Only I can accept your imperfections, realize that "best-before" doesn't mean "use-by," and store you better.

In general, I need to learn more about you because this is about us and our relationship. I help you grow, and then I eat you. Anything else is a waste.

写给食物的情书

（文◎佚名）

亲爱的食物，亲爱的食物，我知道你明白，我需要你。你团聚了我的家庭，你甜蜜了我的庆典，你成就了我的事业，你满足了我的感官，你守护了我的生命。

你拼命让一切成为可能，将一生倾注于生长在田间、工厂或是海洋。我试着对你好些，我给予你一半的土地，三分之二的水，十分之一的能量，以及六分之一的劳动力。但是，我想向你致歉。因为此后你本应被吃掉。但是我扔掉了将近一半的你，其能量足够喂养 1.5 亿人。

从收获到购买回家，我浪费了一半的水果、蔬菜、海鲜，以及三分之一的谷物。我更适于肉类和奶类，只浪费 20%，但这又是双重浪费，本质上说，我排泄的是动物们吃下的谷物或草来产生的肌肉或奶。我浪费的方式很多，比如，有时弃你于田中，任你死去，因为，收割的花销大于你的价值。

有时，我不小心伤害、污染或者落下你。或者因不完美而抛弃你，因为我以貌取物。更多的时候我在超市餐厅和家里将你浪费，而你离被消耗如此之近。我提供得太多，因此，我索取过多却无法吃完，或者我没法在变质前将你卖尽。在家中，我将你抛之脑后或者做了太多却不知如何将你储藏。

也可能，我只是讨厌残羹剩饭。部分问题在于把金额均摊下来，我在你身上的开销并不高，相较于任何国家或任何时期，我的花销被平摊在数天数周内，因此，我并未留意浪费你的代价。但是如果把支出量叠加起来：我将四倍于加利福尼亚的土地以及超过所有非农业用水的总和用于种植不被吃下的食物。

这不是你的错，而是我的。我须买得更少，吃下更多自己所买的。我须接受你的不完美，明白“保质期”并非“可食用期”，并更好地将你储藏。

总而言之，我需要更了解你，因为这关乎我们以及我们的关系。我助你生长，之后将你吃下。除此之外的都属浪费。绘英语

A Love Letter to Durians

（文◎ Thomas Fuller）

When my friend Bob Halliday thinks about durians, the tropical fruit that some say smells like garbage, he not only salivates with delighted anticipation, but he also "foams like a geyser." Those were the words he used on the eve of our visit to an orchard north of Bangkok that was filled with these green spiky fruits dangling dangerously from towering trees.

I confess to the same passion with what must be the world's smelliest fruit.

What is it about the durian? Shaped like a rugby ball with large thorns that can pierce even the most callused hands, durian stinks so badly that it's banned from airplanes, hotels and mass transit in most Southeast Asian cities.

Yet aficionados like Bob and I will travel terrible distances, cancel important appointments—do anything—to scarf down globs of custardy flesh from a durian. While many Thais like their durians harvested early so the interior is

still hard and can be neatly handled, I like an over-ripened durian, which has the consistency of cottage cheese. It's a very messy affair.

It goes without saying that durian is a polarizing and controversial fruit. There is a long tradition of durian haters who cannot get past the smell and gooey-ness of durian, especially among Western visitors to Southeast Asia. Simon de La Loubère, a French diplomat who came here in the 17th century and wrote with unusual empathy about the Kingdom of Siam, drew the line at durian, describing it as "unbearable"because of its smell.

But as a foreign correspondent for nearly two decades, who has always sought to write fairly and dispassionately, I dispense with objectivity for a moment and attempt an ode to what the Malaysians rightly call the king of fruits.

Yes, I freely admit that when ripe it can smell like a dead animal. Yes, the fruit is difficult to handle, bearing likeness to a medieval weapon. But get down to the pale yellow, creamy flesh, and you'll experience overtones of hazelnut, apricot,caramelized banana and egg custard. That's my attempt at describing durian. But words fail;there is no other fruit like it. Bob compares it to the works of Olivier Messiaen,the 20th-century French omposer:complex,dissonant, but with an overall impression of sweetness.

The first time I ted durian was when I was posted in Kuala Lumpur 15 years ago. Trucks piled high with the fruit would come in from the Malaysian countryside, and I would spend evenings sitting with friends on plastic stools by the roadside

sampling different varieties. Unlike the Thais, who cut durians down from trees, Malaysians usually wait for them to fall. The result is a much riper and stronger-tasting durian, sometimes slightly fermented. Durian farmers in Malaysia have been known to wear helmets: No one wants to be on the receiving end of a five-pound spike bomb.

We live in a time when chemists and cooks have joined hands to concoct foods of unrivaled complexity, in everything from packaged snack food to wallet-crushing meals at Michelin-starred restaurants.

What I love about durians is that there is no laboratory needed to achieve the depth and range of tastes they offer. It's one of nature's masterpieces,dangling tantalizingly in the jungle. Durians, even those harvested from the same branch, can be so nuanced and dissimilar that tasting them is something akin to sampling fine wine.

Bob, one of the foremost experts on the food of Thailand, who has written restaurant reviews there for decades,"It tastes like something that was prepared in a kitchen, not grown on a tree," he said after sampling a particularly delightful durian.

Durian season starts in May and tapers off around November in Thailand, depending on the latitude. But these days orchard owners have managed to coax the fruit from trees year round. They are prized by the Thai elite, who offer gan yao durians,a delectable variety with a long stem, as gifts to business partners One fruit can easily sell for $50.

Durians also grow in Malaysia,Indonesia,the Philippines and other parts of Southeast Asia. In Malaysia, the season extends until around the end of the year.

Bob and I recently traveled to three places around Bangkok to sample durian: a high-end Bangkok fruit market; roadside stalls in Chinatown,where durian lovers can get their fix year round until the wee hours ofthesteamy Bangkok night; and the durian orchard outside Bangkok, cherished by durian groupies for its more than two dozen varieties and 300 trees.

Durian is a very social fruit, usually eaten among friends. But I confess that I have sometimes eaten durian alone. Like eating birthday cake by yourself or drinking a tall boy out of a paper bag in a public park, it feels somewhat sad and illicit, which brings up another point. As any durian fan will tell you, durian and alcohol don't mix.

With every durian season comes stories about people who have collapsed—or worse—when they've had large quantities of durian and alcohol. I have never read or heard of a scientific explanation for this, if there is one. But it is widely recognized that durian season can be deleterious to your health. A few years ago, after a routine physical checkup, I was told by my doctor that my triglycerides, a type of fat in the blood, were above normal. She gave me a pamphlet in which the first piece of advice was to cut down on durian or avoid it altogether.

But many of my fellow durian-loving friends are getting along in age, and it reassures me that, well, they are still alive. There are, after all, much more dangerous foods to consume than durian. Blowfish comes to mind.

After a recent and particularly indulgent durianeating marathon, when we felt like rolling away instead of walking, Bob quoted William Blake."The road of excess leads to the palace of wisdom."

给榴梿的情书

（文◎托马斯·富勒）

当我的朋友鲍勃·霍里德想起榴梿——那种被某些人形容为闻起来一股垃圾臭味的热带水果，他不光会满心欢喜，口水直冒，他简直就是“垂涎三尺”。在我们去曼谷北边一处果园参观的前一夜，他就是这么说的。那果园里到处都是这些绿色的长满粗刺的水果，在高耸的果树上摇摇欲坠，很是惊险。

我承认，对于这种绝对是世界上最臭的水果，我有着和鲍勃一样的热情。

榴梿到底长什么样儿？它的形状像一个插满粗刺的英式橄榄球，手上最厚的老茧也能被它刺穿。由于榴梿恶臭非常，大多数东南亚城市都禁止携带榴梿上飞机、进酒店以及搭乘公共交通工具。

然而，像鲍勃和我这样的榴梿“发烧友”，会不远万里，取消重要的约定——任何事——只为了能狼吞虎咽地吃下一团团软嫩香滑的榴梿果肉。虽然很多泰国人喜欢提前采摘榴梿，这样里面的果肉依然硬实，易于处理，但我更喜欢像农家奶酪一样浓稠的熟透榴梿。不过吃起来就要弄得一团糟了。

不用说，榴梿是一种两极分化、富于争议的水果。讨厌榴梿的人有一个悠久的传统，他们无法忍受榴梿的臭味和黏糊糊的口感，这种情况在到东南亚造访的西方游客中尤为严重。在 17 世纪来到此地的一名法国外交官西蒙·德·拉·卢贝尔，他曾带着不同寻常的同理心来描写暹罗王国，却也与榴梿划清界限，称这种难闻的水果“让人无法忍受”。

但作为一名从业近 20 年的外国通讯记者，在写作时我总是努力寻求公正客观，如今我却要暂时放下客观性，来为被马来西亚人尊称为“水果之王”的榴梿唱上一曲赞歌。

不错，我坦率地承认，榴梿成熟时，闻起来可能像是动物的死尸。不错，这种水果的外形像一件中世纪武器一样，棘手得很。但当你尝到了那淡黄色的、奶油状的果肉，你会体验到榛果、杏仁、焦糖香蕉和鸡蛋奶油冻的混合滋味。我尝试如此形容榴梿，不过还是难以言表。没有其他哪种水果能与榴梿媲美了。鲍勃将其比作20世纪法国作曲家奥利弗·梅西安的作品：复杂、刺耳，但整体感受却很甜蜜。

我第一次吃榴梿是15年前被派往吉隆坡的时候。载着堆积如山的榴梿的卡车会从马来西亚农村开进城里，我会整晚整晚地和朋友们坐在马路边的塑料板凳上品尝不同种类的榴梿。这里不像泰国，不会把榴梿从树上割下来，马来西亚人通常会等到它们自己成熟后掉下来。因此这里的榴梿熟得更透，口味也更重，有时候都有点儿发酵了。大家都知道马来西亚的榴梿农户要戴头盔——谁也不想被一个5磅（约2千克）重的带刺炸弹击中。

在我们生活的这个时代，化学家和厨师们携手调制出了无比复杂的食物，既有包装零食，也有米其林星级餐厅里那些昂贵的美食。

我之所以喜欢榴梿就在于，它们所展现的味道的深度和广度无须经过化学实验就能达到。这是一种自然的杰作，就那么撩人地挂在丛林的枝头上。即使是出自同一根树枝上的榴梿，味道也会有些微妙的不同，品尝它们就像品尝好酒一样。

鲍勃是研究泰国食物的顶级专家之一，他写当地的餐馆评论已有数十年。“它就像是从厨房做出来的食物一样，而不像是从树上长出来的。”在尝完一个特别好吃的榴梿后他如此说道。

在泰国，根据纬度的不同，榴梿季从5月开始一直延续到11月。不过现在，果园主们已经把这种果树改造成全年产果了。榴梿受到泰国精英阶层的追捧。他们把“长茎”榴梿，一种长有长茎的美味榴梿品种，作为礼物送给生意伙伴。一个这种榴梿能轻易卖到50美元的价格。

马来西亚、印度尼西亚、菲律宾以及东南亚其他国家和地区也有榴梿出产。在

马来西亚，榴梿季一直延续到年底。

最近，鲍勃和我去了曼谷附近的三个地方品尝榴梿：曼谷的一处高端水果市场；热浪蒸腾的曼谷，中国城的路边摊，榴梿爱好者们一年到头都可以在那里解馋，直至深夜；还有曼谷城郊的一处榴梿果园，那里深受榴梿粉丝的珍爱，因为园中种植了超过二十个品种的三百多棵榴梿树。

榴梿是一种社交性很强的水果，通常是和朋友一起分享的。不过我承认，我有时会独自一人吃榴梿。就像是自己一个人吃生日蛋糕，或者一个人在公园里偷偷从纸袋里拿一罐高罐啤酒出来喝一样，显得有点儿既伤感又偷偷摸摸。这让我想起另一件事。每一个榴梿爱好者都会告诫你，吃榴梿时别喝酒。

每个榴梿季都会传出关于有人吃下大量榴梿又喝了太多酒而病倒的故事，甚至还有更严重的后果。我确实从没读到或听说过关于这种说法的科学解释。不过有件事已被广泛认同：榴梿季可能对你的健康造成伤害。几年前，在一次常规体检后，医生告诉我，我的甘油三酯——血液中的一种脂肪——超标了。她给了我一本医嘱小册子，上面的第一条建议就是：少吃榴梿或者不吃榴梿。

但是我那些同样爱吃榴梿的朋友都一年年安然度岁。嗯，他们都还活着，这让我重拾信心。毕竟，世上还有比榴梿要危险得多的食物呢。我头脑中冒出了河豚。

在我们最近一次纵情享受榴梿盛宴之后，当时我们像是滚着，而不是走着离开的，鲍勃引用了威廉·布莱克的名言：“离经叛道是通向智慧之宫的必由之路。”

A Bite of World:

Top 8 Street Food

（文◎ Anonymous）

Not all great meals come from restaurants. Some are served from stalls and eaten on the go. So called street food is not only delicious, but can be found in nearly every country, rich or poor, " It's a way to get to know the people and the flavor of a place." says Diamanti, an Italian writer, who has nibbled her way around the globe. She shares some her favorite snacks and snaking places.

1.Naples, Italy: Pizza

Pizza may be the closest thing to a global food,but Diamanti says there's nothing like the way it's prepared in Naples. The dish is often ordered from a window counter and quickly baked for customers. If you are eating it on the go,you fold it up for pizza; literally wallet style. "Our pizza is quick and simple." she says.

2.New York,USA: Hot dogs

When foreigners first visit America,one of the first thing smany want to try is the country's typical food,the hot dog." It's the flag for America—both in expensive and democratic,"Diamanti says. "You expect to see kids queuing at a hot dog stall,but it's executives people with ties and suits."

3.Jemaa el-Fna Square, Marrakech, Morocco: Food stalls

When the sun begins to set,this central square comes to life as crowds gather to sing,dance and eat. Hundreds of stalls serve grilled meat,chicken and rice,and the traditional tagine (a spicy Moroccanstew made with

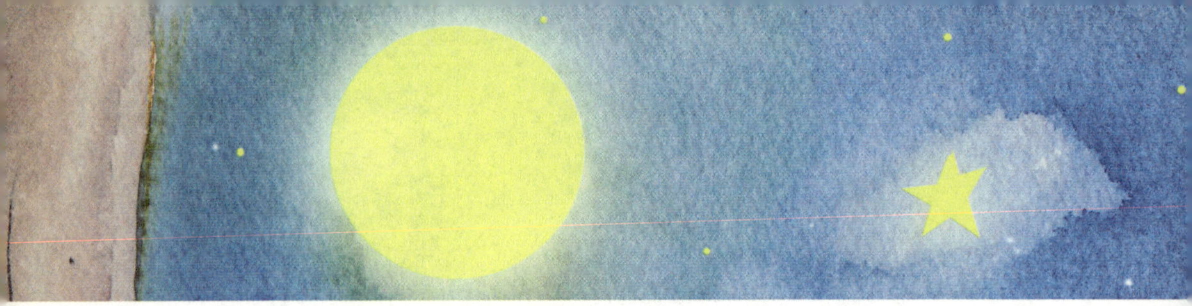

fruit), vegetables and meat. "There is plenty of smoke with hundreds of people cooking at the same time."Diamanti says.

4.Japan: Bento boxes

Diamanti says the best time and place to eat this portable Japanese meal is under a blooming cherry tree in spring. Bento boxes are divided into small compartments, each filled with a different dish: often fish, meat, pickled vegetables, rice or tofu."It really taste delicous." she says.

5.Quebec, Canada: Maple taffy

This seasonal treat is made by boiling maple sap and then quickly harden it on snow or ice. It then is eaten on a stick or fork. This treat can be purchased from sugar shacks near Montreal and in the Laurentian Mountains.

6.Turin, Italy: Aperitifs

This northern Italian city develops vermouth, a fortified wine mixed with spices, and today it's a favorite aperitif. Crowds fill downtown bars before dinner and overflow into the streets. "You take your drink and snack and you go out and chat with friends." Diamanti says.

7.Jordan: Coffee

Diamani spent 15 years working for travel companies in Jordan, and grew to love the coffee which is mixed with cardamom and has a bitter taste. In the desert, it is served by Bedouins, and considered a symbol

of hospitality. "It's offered in small cups without handles." she says. Traditionally, travelers are served three cups. "If a fourth is offered, just shake your cup side to side to indicate you've had your fill ." she says.

8.France： Creepes

These delicate Pancake originated in Brittany,but are now found across France,and beyond. They're prepared on the street and are popular with workers and tourists. Diamanti likes the sweet one,sometimes filled with Nutella, jam or bananas and chocolate with cream.

舌尖上的世界：盘点全球8大街头美食

（文◎佚名）

并非所有的美食都是从餐厅里获得，有些是在摊位上买的，并在路上吃的。所谓的街头食物，不仅味道鲜美，而且几乎在每一个国家都能找到，不论富国还是穷国。“这是一种了解当地人和味道的方式。”意大利作家迪亚曼蒂说。她已经吃遍全球各地，她分享了一些她最爱的小吃以及售卖这些小吃的地方。

1. 意大利那不勒斯：比萨

比萨可能是最接近全球食品的食物了，但迪亚曼蒂说没有哪里像那不勒斯那样制作的。食物往往是从一个窗口柜台订购，并很快为顾客烘烤好。如果你在路上吃，你把它折叠起来，表面看上去就像一个钱包。“那里的比萨饼的特点是快速简单。”她说。

2. 美国纽约：热狗

当外国人第一次来到美国，第一件事情就是想试一下这个国家典型的休闲食品：热狗。“这是美国的标志——既便宜又民主，”迪亚曼蒂说，“你以为会看到孩子们在一个热狗窗口排着队，但看到的却全是那些穿着西装打着领带的管理层。”

3. 摩洛哥马拉喀什马夫纳广场：路边摊

当太阳落下，随着人群聚集到一起唱歌、跳舞以及吃东西时，这个中心广场就开始生气勃勃了。上百个摊位提供烤肉、鸡肉和米饭，以及传统的塔吉锅：一种由水果、蔬菜和肉类做成的辛辣的摩洛哥炖菜。“由于数百人同时做饭，有大量的烟雾弥漫。”迪亚曼蒂说。

4. 日本：盒饭

迪亚曼蒂说，吃这种便携式日本料理的最佳时间和地点是在春天盛开的樱花树

下。饭盒被划分成小隔间，每一格里装满了不同的菜：通常是鱼、肉、腌制蔬菜、米饭或豆腐。“这真的很美味。”她说。

5. 加拿大魁北克：枫糖

这种季节性食品是由沸腾的枫树液迅速在雪地或冰里凝固而制成的。然后，用棍子或者叉子插着吃。这种零食可以从蒙特利尔和劳伦山脉附近的糖窝棚里买到。

6. 意大利都灵：开胃酒

这个意大利北部城市盛产苦艾酒，一种和香料混合的强劲酒，现在它是最受欢迎的开胃酒。晚饭前，人们聚集到市中心的酒吧，街上到处是人。“你拿着你的小酒和零食，出去和朋友聊天。”迪亚曼蒂说。

7. 约旦：咖啡

迪亚曼蒂在约旦的旅行公司工作了１５年，她从小就喜欢这种混合着小豆蔻且有一点儿苦味的咖啡。在沙漠中，它由贝都因人提供，并被认为是一种热情好客的象征。“它用无柄小杯盛着。”她说。传统上，会给游客提供三杯。她说：“如果再给你第四杯，只要左右摇摇你的杯子以暗示‘你够了’。”

8. 法国：薄饼

这种薄饼起源于布列塔尼，但现在在法国境内随处可见。它们在大街上制作，在工人和游客之中很受欢迎。迪亚曼蒂喜欢甜的那种，有时涂着花生酱，果酱，或香蕉、巧克力和奶油。

Mastering the Art of the New York Eat and Walk

（文◎ Anonymous）

It started with a hot dog and a pair of rollerblades. At thirteen years old my version of being a reckless adolescent involved skidding down Broadway on a Saturday afternoon with my best friend, dodging pedestrians while munching on a Gray's Papaya hot dog.

The rollerblades have long since been abandoned— as has my taste for Gray's Papaya, along with other mystery meats— but what remains is my love of eating and walking, at the same time and hopefully with few accidents. Like many favored pastimes, it is difficult to pinpoint its exact appeal. All I know is that it brings together two of my favorite diversions: food and mindless urban wandering. This is not an activity to be undertaken in just any city. It requires a place where you can order any meal to-go, a place where food is shoved into mouths absolutely anywhere and at any time, a place where public eating knows no bounds. On the crowded streets, eating while walking becomes a kind of sidewalk ballet. And no city is more conducive to this dance than New York, where eat-walking is not only normal, but encouraged. And I am a high achiever.

I have always felt that walking while eating is one of the highest

forms of respect you can pay to a food and to a city, and to my city in particular. Tuck into that tub of chicken wings with hot sauce, bite into that impossibly juicy burger, devour that fully-loaded pizza as you walk down the street like it's your last meal — nobody cares. Some call this bad manners. I call this freedom.

When I was nine years old, my mother towed me around Paris for two weeks on a budget that left room for Rodin sculpture viewing, a fair amount of onion soup eating and not much else. All my mother and I wanted come lunchtime was a sandwich to go. The French were not very obliging. Lunch was to be eaten at a table over the course of an hour or so with fixed attention and proper cutlery. A decade later I returned as a college student for a year that was largely spent traveling, in between which I would attend classes and attempt to write papers on the French Surrealists with the crutch of a heavily worn dictionary.

Mostly though, I stomped around the great cities of Europe, specializing in getting lost. I would start in the morning and walk all day, stumbling across a famous church here, an impressive monument there and untangling how one neighborhood flowed into the next. But getting food to go was a challenge. Curry wurst in Vienna, gelato in Florence, kebabs in London— the options were limited and I was only vaguely aware of how gauche it was to walk down the street while snacking on oily chunks of meat. By this time Paris was experiencing the devastating arrival

of le sandwich (on baguettes, naturally). They were sold everywhere— at little kiosks, and stacked neatly in bakery windows with Camembert and charcuterie draping off the sides. They were even thoughtfully wrapped for your portable gastronomic needs. Still, I did not see Parisians walking down the street eating sandwiches like I did. If you had to eat outside you were to sit yourself down on the steps of some great cathedral and nosh away.

The Gallic reverence for food is a bit shattering to the efficiency-minded. Put simply: "Food is good. Eating is not a matter of ingesting calories." So says André Gayot , a food critic, president of Gayot.com and publisher of the *Gayot* guidebooks. He was one of the French critics who attempted to breathe new life into the country's cuisine in the 1960s through coining and promoting nouvelle cuisine, a lighter, stripped-down approach to classic cooking. Despite modern influences on culinary traditions, there remains a sense of celebration at French meals. "We don't like to eat and run," says Gayot, "Work is one thing, and eating is another. It is a moment of reflection and socializing, and a moment of pleasure, like reading a good book or listening to music you like. Even with a busy life, people want to keep this tradition."

Gastronomical reverence aside, animalistic habits are making some inroads in Paris. On my most recent visit earlier this year, I discovered that Parisians had discovered the bagel I did not attempt to try one, mostly out of deference to the French. The sandwich has so deeply infiltrated

lunchtime cuisine in Paris that bagels are this very moment being subjected to supporting multiple kinds of jambon and sacrilegious leafy greens, to the horror of Nova lox everywhere. Back in New York we have been paying equal respect to tradition for years by giving croissants the same treatment. Despite our culinary differences, it seems that American and French lunch-goers share a common desperation for new sandwich bread. And it's having an effect. I spied a few efficient Parisian souls eating sandwiches while marching down cobblestoned streets.

For most New Yorkers, eat-walking is an irresistible trifecta of efficiency: nourishment, exercise and transportation. But for me, it has an opposite appeal. I don't strive for French gastronomic serenity, but rather for a certain clarity that comes with engaging multiple senses at once. I begin to notice things when I slow my gait so as not to choke on a steaming samosa. Sheathed in the act of eating, the city both washes over me and flows through me. With the privilege of distance, scents become sharper, overheard conversations somehow become more profound, people's outfits more interesting, the shiny new glass monolith more elegant and the stew of pedestrians more harmonious. As is the New York way, no one notices the trail of peas and potatoes in my wake. The streets of New York have always been bastions of eccentric indulgences. I weave through a thin crowd wearing a curried smile. I am home.

纽约范儿之 边走边吃

（文◎佚名）

我得从一个热狗和一双轮滑鞋讲起。13 岁时，我还是个冒冒失失的小丫头，经常在周六下午跟我最要好的朋友一起沿着百老汇大街一路滑行，一边躲闪着路上的行人，一边大嚼着从格雷木瓜店里买来的热狗。

如今那双轮滑鞋早就被扔了——对格雷木瓜店里的热狗和其他搞不清成分的肉类食品我也早没了兴趣——但我对边走边吃依然热情不减。跟人们喜欢的很多消遣一样，我很难准确说出它的吸引力到底在哪儿。我只知道它融合了我的两大乐趣：吃东西和漫无目的地在城里闲逛。不是在哪个城市都能这么做的，能这么做的地方需要满足以下条件：在那里，买任何吃的都能带走，无论何时何地都能往嘴里塞东西吃，在公共场合吃东西丝毫不受限制。在拥挤的街头，边走边吃成了在人行道上上演的芭蕾。没有哪个城市比纽约更利于进行这种舞蹈了，在这里，边走边吃的行为不但正常，而且受到鼓励。我就是这方面的高手。

我一向认为边走边吃是向食物和城市表达敬意的最高形式之一，对我所在的城市来说尤其如此。你走在街上，拿着一桶蘸了辣酱的鸡翅大快朵颐，或是咬一口味美多汁到不可思议的汉堡，或是举着块馅料丰富的比萨狼吞虎咽，仿佛这是你的最后一餐——没有人会在乎。有人管这叫没规矩，我管这叫自由。

在我 9 岁时，妈妈拉着我在巴黎转了两个星期。我们的预算有限，除了参观罗丹的雕塑作品和吃好多顿洋葱汤的钱之外所剩无几。到了午饭时间，我和妈妈只想买个三明治在路上吃。法国人在这方面却不怎么与人方便。吃顿午饭得在餐桌边坐上一个来钟头，专心致志地吃，还得恰当地使用餐具。十年后，我以大学生的身份重返巴黎留学一年，我把这一年的大部分时间都花在了旅游上，在旅游的间隙会去上课，然后借助一本被翻烂的词典努力写与法国超现实主义作家有关的论文。

不过，大多数时间我都是在欧洲各大城市暴走，迷路成了我的“专长”。我会

从早上出发，走上一整天，一会儿在这儿发现一座著名教堂，一会儿在那儿看见一座雄伟的纪念碑，一路上研究着一个街区如何与下一个街区会合。但是买外卖食物却是一项挑战。维也纳的咖喱香肠、佛罗伦萨的冰淇淋、伦敦的烤肉串——可供选择的种类有限，而我也只是隐约感到一边吃着油汪汪的大肉块一边走在街上是多么不雅。此时，巴黎正在遭受三明治的大举入侵。到处都有卖三明治的，店家甚至还会贴心地将它包好，方便你拿在路上享用美食。不过，我还是没看到巴黎人像我那样一边在路上走一边吃三明治。如果你不得不在外边吃东西，你得找个大教堂的台阶坐下，然后再开吃。

在效率至上的人看来，法国人对食物的敬畏有些令人诧异。简而言之："食物是好东西。吃东西不是为了摄取卡路里。"说这话的是美食评论家、加约网站总裁、"加约指南"系列图书的出版商安德烈・加约。20 世纪 60 年代，一批法国评论家开始创造和推广比传统烹饪更加清淡和朴素的新式烹饪法，试图以此为法餐注入新的活力，加约便是其中的一员。尽管烹饪传统受到现代社会的影响，但法国人在就餐时依然保持着一种仪式感。"我们不喜欢边吃边走，"加约说，"工作是一码事，吃饭是另一码事。吃饭是进行思考和与别人交流的时刻，是享受快乐的时刻，就像是读一本好书或是听自己喜欢的音乐一样。即使生活忙碌，人们也想保持这个传统。"

撇开对美食的尊重不谈，动物那般的饮食习惯开始侵蚀巴黎。今年早些时候，我最近一次造访巴黎时，发现巴黎人已开始吃贝果了。我没尝试去买，这主要是为了表示对法国人的尊重。在巴黎，午餐吃三明治已经深入人心，眼下连贝果也到处被拿来夹上各种火腿和绿叶蔬菜，甚至夸张到用它夹着烟熏鲑鱼吃。而在纽约，多年来我们也给予了羊角面包相同的待遇，以此向(吃三明治的)传统表达同等的敬意。尽管饮食方面存在差异，但似乎美国人和法国人对于解决午餐抱有共同的渴望——

开发新的三明治面包。而这已在产生效果。我就看见几个讲求效率的巴黎人一边在鹅卵石铺成的街道上大步行走，一边吃三明治。

对于大多数纽约人而言，边走边吃从效率上看一举三得，令人无法抗拒：补充了营养，锻炼了身体，满足了交通需求。但对我而言，它的吸引力刚好与之相反。我并不力求像法国人那样从容地用餐，而是想要获得同时运用多种感官所带来的某种清晰的认知。在我放慢脚步以免被热气腾腾的油炸三角饺噎着时，我开始留意周边的事物。这座被吃的行为所包围的城市既让我无动于衷，又让我深受触动。有了距离这个优势，气味变得更加强烈，无意中听到的对话也不知不觉变得更加深刻，人们的穿着显得更有意思，崭新闪亮的玻璃幕墙显得更加优雅，街上拥挤的人流也变得更加和谐。正如纽约一贯的做派，没人注意到我身后撒落的豌豆和土豆屑。纽约的街道向来是容纳古怪嗜好的堡垒。我面带微笑，嘴里散发着咖喱的气息，穿行在稀拉的人群中。我到家了。

第4章
走在我身边，做我的朋友

You Will Be Alone on the Road of Growth

（文◎ Anonymous）

We're like the cream. When the cream rises to the top, it separates itself from the milk. Perhaps that is what the New Age Movement is really all about. We tell ourselves that it's lonely at the top. Yes, it is. Maybe we have to figure out how to maintain ourselves as cream, but also stay whipped up within the milk? Often, we find ourselves unable to find those other rare individuals who are choosing the same path as ours. The path of sloppy and lazy is full of other people to meet and talk to. The path of whiners is full. The path of being safe, generic, and boring is so crowded you almost cannot even move forward.

Isn't that why you left that path? You had a need to move forward, a need for some elbowroom, a need to spread your arms wide, a need to be seen as special, unique, different. The masses may admire you, but they are not going to be able to really relate to you. You will be alone much of the time.

Do not be afraid of the loneliness of enlightenment. Do not force others to agree with you. Simply give your heart and know that you are growing and that they are free to grow or not. It is the nature of the game.

成长路上的孤独

（文◎佚名）

我们就像奶油。当奶油漂浮到顶部的时候，就会和牛奶分离。也许这种现象就如同新世纪运动的写照。我们发现自己飞得越高，就越感到孤独。是的，现实就是如此。可能我们需要想办法，才能既做好奶油，又不和

牛奶脱离。很多时候，我们很难找到那些选择和我们同路的人。那条潮湿、慵懒的道路挤满了可以相遇并一起聊天的人。那条充满牢骚者的道路上也拥挤不堪。那条所谓安全、普通以及枯燥的道路是如此拥挤以至于你无法向前挪步。

难道这不正是你离开那条道路的原因吗？你需要向前挪步，需要活动的空间，需要展开你的双臂，需要被大众认为你特别，有个性，与众不同。所有的人都仰慕你，但他们却不可能真正地融入你。大部分时间里，你将是孤独的。

不要害怕因认识深而产生的孤独感。没有必要勉强别人欣赏你。做你自己，肯定你自己的成长，别人是否愿意成长就由他们自己决定吧。这就是人生游戏的规则。绘英语

Moonlight Girl and Sunshine Boy

（文◎ Anonymous）

I stumbled across Justin's online dating profile while waiting for water to boil. It was just after 4 a.m.

"Message me if you want to talk about anything and everything until the wee hours of the night," his profile said.

The phrase "wee hours." as it turns out, means different things to different people. I have a circadian rhythm disorder called delayed sleep phase syndrome. It's that my circadian clock tells me it's time for bed when the sun is rising and time to wake up as it's setting. As a vampire, basically offset from society's clock by approximately eight hours.

Now, as a freelance writer making my own schedule, going to bed around 8 or 9 a.m. And waking around 4 or 5 p.m.

Alone with my books and my thoughts, i write about physics. The dark of night is perfect for contemplating the universe. With everything silent and still, it's easier to notice the cracks in reality's facade.

Of course, my chronologic freedom comes with a few technical difficulties, such as an inability to take calls from editors, listen to music without headphones or remember what a day of the week it is, since my days are always changing in the middle.

Then there's dating.

On my first date with Justin, we went to an art museum at 7 p.m, where we spoke easily about lies and passions, software and string theory. I learned that he had a 9–to–5 job and enjoyed cycling and being "out in the sunshine." i didn't mention that I was midway through a regimen of prescription vitamin D, administered in blitzkrieg doses. "Sunshine" was not in my vocabulary.

For our second date, it was my turn to make plans. "I know you're on a normal human schedule," I texted him, “But the Perseid meteor shower peaks tomorrow night. Want to find a dark spot and watch?"

At mid night, we found a cozy spot by the Charles River and gazed upward. Despite the city lights, we saw three meteors blaze above the Boston skyline.

We talked about starlight, how it had begun its journey thousands of years ago and we were looking back in time. I thought how in a sense that's always true; My now is not the same ash is and never will be. There's always a delay, each of us living in the immediate past of the other, regardless of how tightly he wrapped his arms around my waist. We are all trapped in our own time. The best we can do is try to meet in an imaginary middle.

So that's what we did. He booked us a trip to go night skiing. I made it to the beach in time to feel the sun on my skin. He rigged up a high–powered bike light and took me for a long ride in the summer dark. I ate Thai food for breakfast; he ate pancakes for dinner. However, the constant compromise made for two grumpy, bleary–eyed shells of

human beings. He went back to his hometown in Maineto clear his head. I returned to the night.

One afternoon (i.e., just after midnight), I got an email from him suggesting we try a new approach.

"There is no world we both occupy at the same time." he wrote. "It's an illusion. We don't actually need to find that." Instead of fighting our difference, he said, let's just love each other from across the clock.

As a token of our new living arrangement, I gave Justin an illustrated edition of "The Day Boy the Night Girl," In the story, a witch raises two children in captivity, allowing the boy to see only day and the girl only night. But one day, the boy stays out longer than he's supposed to, and when it gets dark, he becomes terrified. The girl finds him shaking in the garden and tries to comfort him, explaining "how gentle and sweet the darkness is, how kind and friendly, how soft and velvety!"

Since she's wide awake, she promises to watch over him while he sleeps. When the sun rises, he awakens to find that now she's scared, a stranger to the sun, and so he carries her in his arms while she sleeps until dark.

Justin and I figured we would do the same. I always made sure to wake up before he got home from work so we could cook and eat together– his dinner, my breakfast. Then he'd go to bed, and I'd write for hours beneath the moon. Eventually, I would crawl quietly into his arms and we'd dream happily alongside each other – for a few minutes, anyway, before he had to get up.

On weekends, he played guitar, saw friends, soaked in the sunshine, all while I was still dreaming. By the time I dragged myself to the coffee maker, he'd cycled 35 miles and eaten two meals. With the sun setting, he greeted me with a happy "Good morning!" He told me about his day; I told him about my yesterday.

And so it went, the earth spinning for each of us of us in turn. We made the most of the hours when our lives overlapped, then let each other thrive in our own times, like animals in our wilds.

In August, the earth made its annual pass through the dust and debris of that ancient comet. Late that night, Justin drove me to a secluded beach on the north shore of Massachusetts where a handful of stargazers stared skyward. He put down a blanket as frogs croaked in the distance. Then he fumbled in his camera bag, pulling out a small black box. I couldn't see what was inside, just a glint, like the flicker of a star. Then he asked, "will you marry me?"

We lay back on the blanket, grinning, as meteors streaked the sky. By then it was nearly 2 a.m., too late to call anyone, to squeal our news to family and friends. Instead we just lay there in our shared place and time, surrounded by sand and ocean and a few hundred billion stars.

当月光女孩遇见阳光男孩

（文◎佚名）

贾斯汀的在线约会个人主页。当时刚过凌晨四点。

“如果你想探讨任何事情，请发信息给我，凌晨之前都可以。”他在个人主页上写道。

事实证明，在不同的人看来，“凌晨”有着不同的含义。我有昼夜节奏紊乱的问题，即睡眠相位后移综合征。我的生物钟会在日出时告诉我该上床休息了，在日落时告诉我该醒来了。基本就像吸血鬼一样——偏离被社会认可的时钟约八小时。

现在，作为一名自行制订个人日程表的自由撰稿人，我每天早上八九点钟上床，下午四五点钟醒来。

当我书写与物理有关的文字时，唯有我自己的书籍和思想为伴。在暗夜中思索宇宙的奥秘，是再合适不过的。

当然，我在作息方面的自由遭遇了几个技术上的难题，比如无法接编辑打来的电话，无法不戴耳机听音乐，无法记住每一天是星期几，因为我的一天总是从半截儿算起。

还有就是约会。

第一次和贾斯汀约会，我们在晚上七点去了一家艺术博物馆。我得知他有一份朝九晚五的工作，喜欢骑自行车，喜欢沐浴在“户外的阳光里”。我没提及自己正按照医生的处方猛补维生素D，我的词汇表里根本没有“阳光”这个词。

第二次约会时，轮到我制订计划了。“我知道你是一个作息时间正常的人，”我在发给他的信息中写道，“但英仙座流星雨将在明晚达到高潮。想要找个黑暗的角落一起观赏吗？”

午夜时分，我们在查理斯河边找到了一个舒服的地方。尽管城市里闪耀着

灯火，我们还是看到三颗流星在波士顿天际线上方划过。

我们谈论星光，说起它如何于数千年前就踏上旅程，而我们其实是在回望过去。我发现在某种意义上，事情竟然总是如此：我的现在和他的现在不是一回事，而且永远也不会是一回事。延迟永远存在，我们俩都活在对方刚刚度过的时间里，不论他如何紧紧地搂着我的腰。我们都被困在各自的时间里，最好的情况是设法在想象中的钟点碰头。

于是我们这样做了。他为我们俩预定了一趟夜间滑雪的行程。我也及时赶到海滩上，体会了阳光洒在皮肤上的感觉。他给自行车配备了一盏高功率的车灯，载着我在一个夏夜里骑行了好长一段路。我拿泰国风味的食物当早餐，他则拿薄饼当晚餐。

然而，这种持续不断的妥协最终造就了两具脾气暴躁、睡眼惺忪的躯壳。他回到位于缅因州的故乡去厘清思路。我则回归了黑夜。

一天下午（意即午夜过后），他发来一封邮件，建议我们采取一种新的相处模式。

“我们俩同时占据的世界并不存在，”他写道，“它是一种幻觉。我们其实不必寻找它。”与其对抗我们的差异，他说，我们不如隔着时间相爱。

作为我们全新的生活安排的象征，我送给贾斯汀一本插画版《日之少年与夜之少女》，在这个故事里，一个女巫圈养着两个孩子，让男孩只能看到白天，让女孩只能看到黑夜。但有一天，男孩待在外边的时间超出了规定，当天色变暗的时候，他很害怕。女孩发现他在花园里瑟瑟发抖，试图安慰他，向他解释："黑暗是多么温柔甜蜜，多么善良友好，多么柔软光滑！"

由于她正处于完全清醒的状态，于是承诺在他睡觉时看护他。当他在太阳升起之际醒来，发现她正惊魂未定，因为从未见过太阳，于是他让她在自己怀中睡去，直到黑夜降临。

我和贾斯汀认为，我们俩也可以如此行事。我总是确保自己在他下班回家之前起床，这样一来我们就能一同烹饪和进餐——他的晚餐，我的早餐。然后他上床睡觉，我则在月光下写上几个小时。最终，我会悄悄溜进他怀里，我们会一同幸福地进入梦乡——尽管只有几分钟，在他不得不起床之前。

周末，当他弹吉他、见朋友、晒太阳的时候，我仍在梦乡之中。等到我把自己拖到咖啡机前，他已经骑行了 35 公里，吃过了两餐饭。太阳下山时，他会用一句欢快的"早上好"跟我打招呼。接着，他把自己一天的经历讲给我听，我则把自己前一天的经历讲给他听。

就这样，地球轮番为我们俩旋转。我们充分利用了两个人生活中相互重合的那些小时，然后让对方在各自的时间里自得其乐。

到了 8 月份，地球像往年一样，又从那颗古老彗星的尘埃和碎片中经过。当天深夜，贾斯汀开车将我载至马萨诸塞州北海岸一处僻静的沙滩，那里只有不多的几个人在看星星。他就着远处的蛙鸣铺开一条毯子，又在相机包里摸索一番，拿出一个黑色的小盒子。我看不清盒子里装着什么，只看到闪耀的光芒，就好像星星眨着眼睛。然后他问："你愿意嫁给我吗？"

我们仰面躺在毯子上，在流星划过夜空之际咧着嘴笑。当时已经接近凌晨两点，太晚了，不好打电话给任何亲朋好友汇报我们的喜讯。因此我们只是躺在那儿，躺在我们共同的时空里，周围是沙滩、海洋和数不清的星星。

A Best Friend Is Enough

（文◎ Jacquelyn Mitchard）

If you have that one friend, you're rich. That one friend is different from all the others, dear as they may be. I met Jeanine on my first day of high school, more than 35 years ago, at the age of 13. Painfully shy, I had signed up for student council because I thought it might save me from wandering around a huge high school shamefully alone. It was still early in the day. I'd already lost my new green trench coat and couldn't remember which building my locker was in. Standing there in the office, miserable, I wanted to vanish into the paneling.

I heard a girl's voice: "Do you have a lot of friends?"

When I saw her—tiny, delicate, with beautiful eyelashes—I smiled and answered, "Are you kidding? I'm the girl nobody knows."

"Well, I'm nobody." Jeanine said.

That was it. The two of us were instant friends. For the next six years, Jeanine and I spent hours on the phone each weekday and virtually every weekend night together. As boys came and went, we drowned our sorrows in tomato soup. In my mother's old Chevy, we cruised the West Side of Chicago. We sat on Al Capone's grave one Halloween night. Lying on blankets under the stars, we'd talk of our dreams, pouring our hearts out.

Jeanine wanted to sing on the Broadway stage. I wanted to write a novel. "Why not two? Why not five?" she pressed me.

As high school progressed, I became a student council officer and made friends by the score. Jeanine? She preferred the sidelines. She was like the angel in my pocket. I never forsook her, never excluded her. Other friends could not understand our devotion, because we seemed like such opposites. But we weren't.

Neither of us got much attention at home. Jeanine's parents worked long hours. Mine had other fish to fry, and those fish swam at the bottom of a highball glass. I don't think my parents ever attended a single high school event of mine, though my mother made sure I dressed well—she wanted me to be the prettiest girl (and the thinnest).

Jeanine and I remained a sorority of two, and even college didn't intervene. Neither did Jeanine's early unplanned motherhood during our freshman year. After her daughter, Gemma, was born, Jeanine moved back home. My mother, I'm proud to say, offered them both love and support.

Unfortunately, Mama didn't get to play grandma for real. After she was diagnosed with brain cancer and given just a few months to live, I married a boy who was only a pal so she could see me in a wedding gown. When my marriage was quietly annulled, I came home for good, finishing school and working as a waitress to help my younger brother get through high school.

Jeanine and I were together again, this time with a baby seat in the back of the car. We picked up where we left off, the Beach Boys on the radio as we cruised familiar routes.

Then, in my early 20s, I took a coveted job on a Wisconsin newspaper and had to start work every day at 5 a.m. Spent and challenged, I didn't get home often enough to see Jeanine through the terror she felt when her beloved father learned that he, too, had cancer. And when he died, I was too new at my job to take time off for his funeral. The last words Jeanine spoke to me, for four years, were "You betrayed me".

I said thousands of words, through the crack under her apartment door, in letters, in cards, pleading with Jeanine to understand. But she was stubborn and wouldn't forgive me.

When I married for real, Jeanine was not there. When my beloved firstborn son arrived, she wasn't there to be his godmother, as I was to Gemma. And when my second and third sons were born after my struggles with infertility, Jeanine wasn't there either.

But when cancer came to the door again, this time to claim my husband, Dan, Jeanine came, too, unbidden. We didn't talk about the lapse

in our friendship until much later. Suffering through hellish grief, I was simply staggered by gratitude.

I kept thinking, If Jeanine is with me, I can live through this. I can be okay. If Jeanine is holding me, helping me, I am home.

I would never let her go again.

We resumed our marathon phone sessions, dissecting jobs, life, her dates, my lack of them. When others called me foolish, she told me to go ahead, to write my first novel during the two years after Dan died instead of taking a real job. You can do this, she said. All I wanted was to show my sons that no matter the size of the hole life drove through you, you still had permission to live large.

In the end, my novel, *The Deep End of the Ocean*, became the first book ever chosen by Oprah's Book Club. Jeanine cheered—as she did two years later when I married my husband, Chris. And after Jeanine graduated from college with a degree in theater, I cheered for her as she became a sought-after voice and acting teacher, winning roles onstage and in commercials.

Before Jeanine even turned 40, her legs began to hurt. Deep into my aerobics period, I teased her: "It's because you're such a weenie."

She wouldn't work out, but she did stretch, try massage therapy and take vitamins. Then an e-mail from a friend broke the news that Jeanine had been too devastated to speak: She had multiple sclerosis.

Four years ago, I realized that my fierce, beloved friend, dedicated actress that she was, had never seen a Broadway show. Together we went—Jeanine pushing her walker, the two of us wearing our fanciest

sequined skirts—to see her favorite musical, *Man of La Mancha*. When Brian Stokes Mitchell sang of the impossible dream, the unbeatable foe, I had a brainstorm: I could use my small measure of new celebrity to raise money for something, and for someone. Jeanine had helped me craft the heroine of my sixth novel, *The Breakdown Lane*, a dancer who in one harrowing year loses her husband and develops MS. I would donate a portion of the book's sales, and go from there.

Last spring, at an MS fund-raiser in Washington, D.C., I was about to sign books when I heard the old Bill Withers song "Lean on Me." I looked up. There on the screen, larger than life, was a photo of me with my head leaning on Jeanine's shoulder. The coordinator read a letter Jeanine had written: "Jackie was popular; I was the little caboose. But she chose me, included me, and when she learned I had MS, she jumped in to help me beat this disease. She's more than a friend. She's my heart."

That goes for me too. Jeanine has to lean on my arm when we walk. But I have to lean on her a hundred times a year, when I turn to her with problems no one else understands, problems no one else can see me through. As she describes them, they're like locational humor: To get it, you had to be there.

She always was.

有一位挚友就够了

（文◎杰奎琳·米特查德）

假如你拥有一个与众不同的朋友，那就足够了。我认识珍妮是在35年前，那时我13岁。高中的第一天，我极度害羞，不知所措地走向学生委员会签名报到，因为我想这样就可以免于一个人尴尬地在这么大的校园里独自徘徊。那天时间尚早，我不仅丢了新买的绿色雨衣，而且忘记了我的寄物柜所在教学楼的位置。我伤心地站在办公室门口，恨不得消失在门缝里。

这时，我听到一个女孩的声音："你有很多朋友吗？"

当我转过身，看到一个小巧、精致的女孩，长着漂亮的眼睫毛，我冲着她笑笑并回答："你是在开玩笑吗？我可是个没有人认识的女孩。"

"那么，我想我就是那个'没有人'。"珍妮说。

的确如此。从那之后我们成了亲密无间的朋友。在随后的6年中，每天我们俩都会"煲电话粥"，周末差不多都在一起度过；我们把各自的失恋埋葬在自制的西红柿汤里；我们还曾开着我妈的老牌雪佛兰车到达过芝加哥的西区；我们还曾一起坐在阿尔·卡彭的坟墓前度过了一个万圣节的晚上；我们还曾铺上毯子，一起躺在星空下，谈我们未来的梦想以及倾吐心声。

珍妮的梦想是能够成为百老汇舞台上的歌手，而我希望能够写一本小说。"为什么不写2本？5本？"她不断这样激励我。

高中毕业后，我进入地方议会做实习议员，并结交了新的朋友。至于珍妮，她喜欢做兼职，有时会得到我的接济，但我从没有嫌弃过她，躲避过她。我们其他的朋友总是不理解我们之间的友谊，因为他们认为我俩的性格看上去格格不入。其实不然。

我们俩的家庭观念都很淡薄。珍妮的父母工作时间很长，我的父母也有重要的事情要做。我的父母从来都没有参加过我高中时的任何家长会、比赛等等，尽管我的母亲每次都替我打理着装，她希望我是最漂亮的女孩。

珍妮和我一直都是女生联谊会的会员，上大学以后也没有中断，就是在我们上大一那年珍妮出乎意料地当上了妈妈后也没有中断过。在她的女儿吉玛出生后，她搬回家了。我可以毫不夸张地说，我的妈妈那时给予了她很多爱和支持。

不幸的是，我的妈妈却没有能够真正地当上外祖母。当她被诊断得了脑癌并且生命只剩下几个月后，我为了能让妈妈看到我穿婚纱的样子就急匆匆地和一个只是朋友的男孩结了婚。之后我悄悄地解除了婚约，回到家，像一个女佣那样照顾我的弟弟顺利读完高中。

我和珍妮又在一起了，不同的是，这次我们的汽车后座上多了一个婴儿座位。我们一边听着沙滩男孩的歌一边行驶在熟悉的路上，一如从前。

在我 25 岁之前，我在威斯康星报社得到了一份梦寐以求的工作，之后开始有了早上 5 点就工作的上班生活。我不断地付出并随时准备迎接挑战，以至于当珍妮的父亲得了癌症之后，我都没有太多的时间经常回家陪珍妮度过那段难熬的时期。珍妮的父亲死后，我因为工作不久而不被准假去参加他的葬礼。珍妮对我说的最后一句话是：你背叛了我！

我说了数千次道歉的话，还写信、写卡片塞进她公寓的门缝里，请求她的理解，但是她都倔强地拒绝了。

当我真正结婚的时候，她没有出现；当我深爱

的第一个儿子出生后，她也没有像我当初做吉玛的教母那样来当我第一个儿子的教母；当我经历过一段时间的不育后生第二个、第三个孩子时，她仍然没有来看我。

但是当癌症再一次光临并降临在我丈夫丹头上时，珍妮来了。我们在很久以后才谈起我们之间的不和，承受着极大的悲痛，我还是很感谢她的到来。

我不停地想，要是珍妮跟我在一起，那么我会渡过难关，我会好起来。如果珍妮支持我，帮助我，我就有了像家一样的安全感。

我不会再让她离开我了。

我们又开始了马拉松式的电话交谈，聊工作、生活、她的约会以及我的得与失。在丹死后的这两年我想写自己的第一部小说，而不想去找工作。当有人说我愚蠢的时候，珍妮告诉我要坚持。你会成功的，她说。我所要做的，只是告诉我的孩子，无论生活带给你多大的困境，你仍然有权利自由地选择生活。

最终，我的小说 *The Deep End of The Ocean*《海洋深处》成为第一本 Oprah's Book Club（《奥普拉读书俱乐部》节目创办于 1996 年，最初六年，每月推荐一部作品，供观众阅读讨论，每本都成了畅销书。一本书只要在封面贴上《奥普拉读书俱乐部》的标志，便至少能多卖出 50 万本甚至 100 万本。有人说："她就是推荐电话号码簿，人们也会去读。"）推荐的书。珍妮为我庆祝，两年后当我和克里斯结婚时，她也同样为我祝贺，就像当她大学毕业并获得戏剧学位后我为她庆祝那样。她成了最受欢迎的歌手和表演系老师，并且名利双收。

珍妮在 40 岁之后，腿部开始疼痛，我那时每天都坚持做有氧健身操，我开玩笑地说："这是因为你是这样的一个女孩。"

她不能外出工作了，但是她还是做着努力。她做按摩疗法（massage therapy）并补充维生素。不久，一个朋友通过电子邮件告诉我珍妮的病情恶化到不能说话了，她患有多发性硬化症。

四年前，当我意识到我深爱着的这位热忱的女演员好友，还没有看过一次百老汇的演出。于是我们就一起去了。珍妮推着助行架，我俩都穿上各自最喜欢的装饰有闪光小圆片的长裙去看珍妮最喜欢的音乐剧——《梦幻骑士》。当布雷恩·斯托克斯·米切尔唱着遥不可及的梦想，不可战胜的敌人，我突然有了灵感：我可以在我的新书发布会上为一些事、一些人募集资金。珍妮帮助我创作了我的第六本小说 *The Breakdown Lane*《崩溃人生》，书中的女主角是一个舞者，经历了失去丈夫而后患上多发性硬化症痛苦的一年。我将从那开始把我的部分书款用于捐赠。

去年春天，在华盛顿的一个多发性硬化症募集基金会上，当我正要开始签名售书时，我听到了比尔·威瑟斯的歌 *Lean On Me*《信赖我》，我抬起头看大屏幕，那是一张我把头靠在珍妮的肩膀上的照片，画外音响起，那是一封珍妮写的信："杰基（作者的昵称）总是很受欢迎，我只是一节小车厢，但她选择了我，包容我。当她得知我患上多发性硬化症后，她立刻出现在我面前帮我共同战胜疾病。她不只是我的一个朋友，她还是我的心。"

对我也是一样。当我们一起走时，珍妮得扶着我的胳膊，而我总是带着自己那些其他人不能理解的问题，其他人无法使我渡过难关的问题去找珍妮，从这种意义上说，我在一年之中不知要依靠她多少次。正如她描述的那样，那些问题就像是当地的谚语："不入虎穴，焉得虎子。"

她一直如此。

How Did I Get Away the Pain of Being Isolated by My Friends

（文◎ Anonymous）

When reality slaps you really hard I'm sure you'll wake up in pain. That is exactly what happened to me. I must say I'm a good friend. A shoulder to cry on, give you some piece of advice when you need them. Give you surprise when you least expect them. I will never forget every single thing that is special to us.

They said true friends will never leave you. But I wonder why me and my "true friends" are now apart? I've been in this group of friends for four years. But just when I thought we have a strong bond, everything went down. Once they make you feel like they will not be completed without you, next thing you know you are no longer belong. I don't really have an idea why they drift away. I feel rejected in a way that when I try to talk to them they turn their backs.

I feel betrayed in a way that I trusted them

in every single thing, in every single secret that I have then in a snap gossip blows out. I feel depression and loneliness. The people I trusted the most are now the one who's putting me in shame. There comes a time that I skip meals and don't drink anything. I got sick and been confined, but didn't hear a thing from them. There comes a time that I feel empty because no one can understand me. The pangs of anxiety slowly get into me. I tried cutting myself. Did I hear a thing from them? No! They all know that they are the reason behind all this stupidness but I got no reaction from them. Swear they are the sweetest!

But how did I get away with it? I felt so much pain throughout this journey. I felt exhausted and about to give up. I gave up the relationship. I shift my attention to myself; I read more books, talked with my heart by writing dairy. And slowly I recovered with all of the pain and depression. Now that I'm over with all the things they brought me, they started to communicate with me. I know I'll meet more people in the future. But for now, I'll just focus on loving my self more than them. People come and go. There are other things worth our tears and pain. Maybe you're struggling with a big thing right now but always remember your heart is always there to guide us. Nothing is bigger than it! Trust yourself and have faith.

We are all great individual. Don't lose hope no matter how hard the situation is. Life is beautiful live it the way it's supposed to be.

和朋友疏远的那段日子，我怎么挨过

（文◎佚名 译◎ Zeey）

现实一个重重的耳光打过来，你会在疼痛中清醒，就像我一样。必须得说，我称得上“好朋友”这仨字。你哭泣的时候，我给你肩膀依靠；你需要的时候，我会给你建议；有时候给你制造出人意料的惊喜。我从不会忘记任何一件对彼此有特殊意义的小事。

人们常说真正的朋友永远不会离你而去。但为什么我的“挚友”要和我疏远？我们已经做了 4 年的朋友。恰恰在我觉得关系已经密不可分的时候，一切却变得不如以往。以前她们给你这种感觉——没有你，她们的世界就不完整，而当下你会觉得自己是局外人。我当时真的不明白她们为什么会远离我，我试着和她们讲话，但她们会故意转过身去。

我觉得自己被背叛了，我毫无保留地和她们分享，现在这些小秘密却被当成八卦来散布。我感到无助和孤独，我曾信任的人使我陷入羞耻当中。有一段时间我连饭都吃不下。不与人接触，也没有那些“朋友”的消息。那段时间，我感到如此空虚，因为没有人能够理解我这种感觉。这种焦虑慢慢浸染了我，我变得郁郁寡欢。我的朋友们呢？她们当然知道我为啥变成这个蠢样子，但她们无动于衷。

我是怎么挨过这段时间的呢？这段时间，我觉得痛苦万分，筋疲力尽，想要放弃。最后，我放弃了这段关系。我看了很多书，通过写日记来和自己的内心进行交谈。慢慢地，我从那些痛苦和失望里挣脱了出来。我挨过了那段日子，不再为她们的所作所为感到难过，而这时，她们反过来想要和我交流。我知道

在以后我会遇到更多的人。但是现在，我更关注我自己的内心。也许还有很多别的事情，让你和我一样感到痛苦，但请你记住，心是我们的指引。相信自己，你就不会惧怕痛苦。

每个人都是值得骄傲的个体，不管境况多艰难，都不要失去希望，生活还是会一如既往地美好下去。

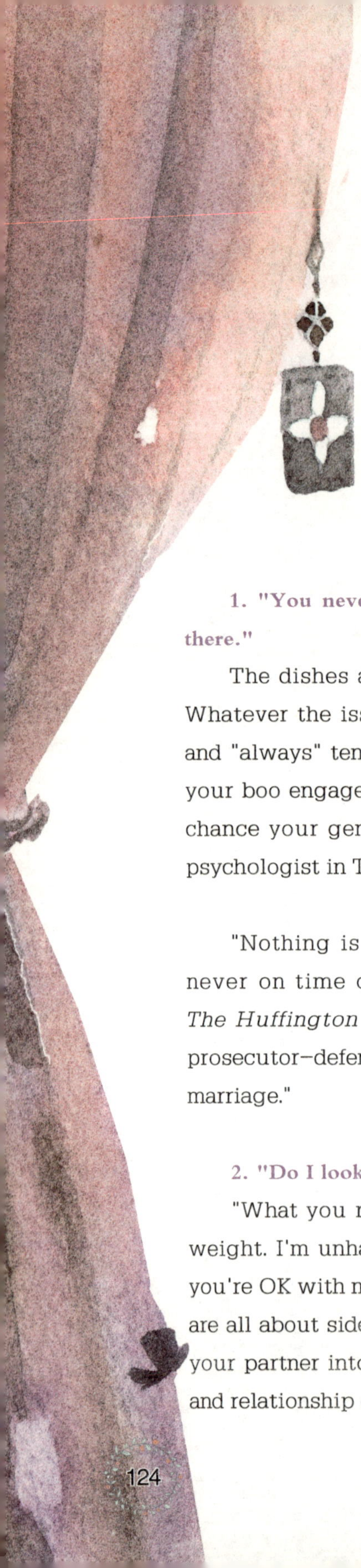

The Most Deadly Phrases In a Relationship

(文◎ Anonymous)

1. "You never do the dishes. You always just leave them sitting there."

The dishes are a placeholder for pretty much anything here. Whatever the issue, using accusatory blanket terms like "never" and "always" tends to end the same way every time: with you and your boo engaged in an overblown argument. Plus, there's a good chance your generalization is wrong, said Samantha Rodman, a psychologist in Takoma Park, Maryland.

"Nothing is black and white so telling a partner that she's never on time or he's always selfish can't be right," she told *The Huffington Post*, "These types of statements only lead to a prosecutor-defendant dynamic, which is not what you want in your marriage."

2. "Do I look like I've put on weight?"

"What you really mean by asking this is, 'I know I've put on weight. I'm unhappy about how I look and I need you to say that you're OK with my current state." she said. "These types of questions are all about side-stepping personal responsibility, plus they force your partner into an enabling role." said Robyn Wahlgast, a dating and relationship coach for women.

3. "Have you put on a few pounds?"

Blunt, negative remarks to your spouse about his or her appearance are also out of line.

"Unconstructive criticism of physical appearance is as bad as it gets."

Whetstone said, "It's painful because you're suggesting that your partner isn't good enough or that they're less than or defective."

4. "You're a horrible parent, breadwinner, lover..."

"Negative statements about our self-identities are devastating. These roles are so important and tender. When they're questioned, we feel completely torn down. It becomes hard to forget statements like this."

5. "Ugh, I hate when you do that." (Said in front of friends or family.)

Putting your spouse down in front of others is a huge no-no in a relationship, said Whetstone.

6. "You shouldn't feel that way."

There's nothing more belittling or condescending than telling your spouse what he should or shouldn't be feeling in any given situation, Rodman said.

"There is no right or wrong way for someone to feel,"

she said. "Feelings are what they are; try to understand your partner and be curious about his experience rather than dismissing what you don't understand."

虽然我们很亲密，我也不应该对你说

（文◎佚名）

1. “你从来都不洗碗，总是把它们扔在那儿就不管了。”

来自马里兰州塔科马帕克的心理学家萨曼莎·罗德曼说，这里的碗碟可以用任何事物代替。无论是什么问题，只要用到“从来不”“总是”等充满指责意味的概括性字眼，每次都会导致同样的结果：你和伴侣大吵一架。而且，你的概括很有可能是错误的。

她对《赫芬顿邮报》说：“没有什么

事是非黑即白的，所以对伴侣说，她从来没有准时过或他总是很自私，并不好。这些话只会导致你们不断来回指责和辩解，这并不是你在婚姻里想要的。”

2. “我是不是胖了？”

“你问这句话的真正意思是‘我知道我体重增加了，我不满意我的样子，我需要你说你对我的现状很满意’。回答这些问题都不是必要的个人责任，而且这种问题相当于在逼迫伴侣去发挥激励你的作用。”女性约会和恋爱辅导师萝宾·沃尔葛斯特如是说。

3. “你是不是胖了？”

直白、消极地评论配偶的外貌也越过了红线。

“毫无助益地批评外貌，要多糟有多糟，”惠茨通说，“这样很伤人，因为你在暗示你的伴侣不够好、差那么一点儿、有缺陷。”

4. “你是个糟糕的家长 / 当家的 / 爱人……”

“消极评价个人身份的结果是毁灭性的。我们的角色重要又脆弱，它们一旦被质疑，我们就感觉完全崩溃了。我们也很难忘掉这样的话。”

5. “呃，我讨厌你那么做。”（当着朋友或家人的面说）

惠茨通说，当着他人的面贬低配偶是婚姻与恋爱关系中万万不可做的事。

6. “你不该那么想。”

罗德曼说，没有什么比告诉你的配偶在某种情况下应该或不应该怎么想更居高临下、更贬低人的了。

她说：“一个人怎么想没有对错，感觉就是感觉，不可捉摸；要试着去理解你的伴侣，询问他怎么得来这样的体验，而不是否认你不理解的事。”

Why Girlfriends Are More Important than Your Boyfriend

（文◎ Anonymous）

1. There's no embarrassment

The number one rule with your best friends: never feel embarrassed to say what's on your mind. You can tell them anything, and I mean anything, and they won't care.

It's probably because they can relate. You're both women, so they know exactly how it feels when your emotions go haywire during that time of the month.

Explaining this to your boyfriend isn't always easy, and for the most part they just don't get it. There's no shame telling your friends about your digestive problems — they totally understand and will never judge you for it.

2. They give great advice

The best advice usually comes from a close relative or your girlfriends. They know you very well, and because they have been through similar situations themselves, they are always there to help you out in your time of need.

You can hardly ask your boyfriend about boy problems— it just wouldn't have the same outcome.

3. They remember the little details

A true best friend will never forget your birthday or other important dates that mean a lot to you. They make it their mission to remember the little things about you: how you two met, your favorite movie, how you like your coffee, and all of the other small details that shape you into the person you are.

Your boyfriend will probably have to be reminded of important dates and will most definitely forget your anniversary.

4. They like the same things

One of the reasons you and your girls get along so well is because

you have a lot in common. They are always down to binge watch *Friends* or *Gossip Girl*, which is really not your boyfriend's kind of thing.

And you can swap clothes. Your girlfriends will tell you what looks good and what doesn't work at all. Your boyfriend will probably just tell you what he thinks you want to hear, rather than the truth.

为何闺蜜比男朋友更重要

（文◎佚名）

1. 没有尴尬

与最好的朋友在一起的第一条法则：说出脑中所想永远都不会感到尴尬。你可以告诉她们你的任何想法，我说的是所有一切，而且她们不会在乎。

可能是因为她们能将心比心，你们都是女人，所以她们能够准确地知道你在每月的那个时候感情发疯的感觉。

和你的男朋友解释这一点往往不容易，而且他们在大多数情况下很难理解。告诉朋友你的消化问题并没有什么害羞的——她们会完全理解你，而且永远不会用这一点来评价你。

2. 她们能给出很好的建议

最好的建议往往来自于最亲近的亲戚或者你的女性朋友。她们很了解你，因为她们自己也经历过类似的情况，她们总是能在你需要的时候帮助你脱离困境。

你几乎不能问你的男朋友关于男孩的问题——结果往往不会相同。

3. 她们会记住小细节

真正的好朋友永远不会忘记你的生日以及其他对你很重要的日子。她们将记住你的这些小细节当作任务来做：你们两个如何认识的，你最喜欢的电影，你喜欢喝什么样的咖啡，以及其他小的细节，这些都是你的特点。

你的男朋友或许需要你提醒他重要的日子，而且很可能会忘记你们的纪念日。

4. 她们喜欢相同的东西

你和你的女性朋友相处得特别好的原因之一就是你们有许多相同点。她们总是放纵地看《老友记》或者《绯闻女孩》，这种电视剧往往不是你的男朋友所喜欢的类型。

而且你们可以交换衣服。你的女性朋友会告诉你怎么穿衣服好看，怎么穿衣服完全不行。你的男朋友很可能会告诉你他认为你想听的话，而不是事实。

How to Treat the Pain of Breakup as Curing Fracture

（文◎ F.Diane Barth）

First, it means recognizing that you are suffering from an injury. These steps toward recovery are based on physician-recommended procedures for healing from a physical injury.

1. Allow yourself time to heal. Get enough rest. And feed yourself well, even if you don't feel much like eating. Food nourishes your body, and this is a time that your body needs nourishment to repair itself.

When you are physically injured, you are often told to stay off of the injured part of your body for a period of time. According to the Mayo Clinic, both mental exertion and a too-soon return to physical activity after a brain injury (such as a concussion) can worsen symptoms and puts the injured

person at risk of potentially permanent damage. The same can be true for the pain of a breakup. Sometimes it seems as though an emotional injury doesn't get credit for being as painful as it is. When there's a physical sign of distress—a cast or a sling or crutches—we get a lot of sympathy. But while people may be sympathetic about the pain of a breakup for a while, they often want us to "get over it" before we're actually are healed. Remind yourself—and maybe gently remind your well-intentioned family or friends—that, like physical injuries, emotional injuries need time.

2. So what's the equivalent of resuming physical activity after a breakup? Dating? Not exactly. That would be like going back to running five miles after you've been off a broken leg for six weeks. Just as with physical exercise, it's important to start back slowly and carefully, to give your body and your psyche a chance to get used to the activity. You need to rebuild your feeling muscles just as you would your physical muscles. Maybe start with a quiet evening with friends, or a drink with an old buddy. See how it feels, and when you feel ready, try a larger social event.

3. When you do start dating again, be prepared for some anxiety and discomfort. It's natural to be guarded in these situations. You're going to have a fear of being hurt again. Slow and easy is the way to move forward, just as you would if you were increasing your exercise regimen after hurting yourself. I actually encourage people I work with to share with dates that they are just getting over a breakup. Some counselors disagree with this advice, but my thinking is that saying it gives you a little more leeway to go even more slowly. It's like saying that you just got a cast taken off your leg, so you can't run full out right now. It doesn't mean you won't be able

to in the near future. Sure, it might scare some potential dates away; but my feeling is that they might not have been the best match for you at this point in your recovery anyway.

4. Eventually, you will notice that you are genuinely feeling better. One danger of this stage is that you may have gotten too comfortable in your recovery position. Maybe you're afraid to take a chance. Maybe you've gotten comfortable feeling sorry for yourself or focusing on your anger at your old partner. These thoughts and feelings can keep you stuck, when you're actually ready to move on. Some honest soul-searching can help you move on. Are you afraid of repeating old patterns? Are you ready to make some changes in how you approach dating and relationships? Use this time to assess your real hopes and desires about a relationship. Now is a good time to make a realistic appraisal of what went wrong with the relationship that just ended. Did you miss early signs that something was amiss? Can you take responsibility for your own part in the difficulties? What can you do differently this time? And what can you ask from your next partner that maybe you didn't let yourself put out there with the last one?

5. Once you have healed, let go of the old relationship. You're ready to move toward a new one, but chances are good that you won't encounter the "right" person immediately. Take advantage of the opportunity to meet new people—maybe some you wouldn't have ever gotten to know otherwise. Learn something new and return to old pleasures. Don't make snap decisions and don't jump into something just because it feels comfortable—or because it feels different.

6. Remember that injuries can lead to growth and new directions. Take your healthy heart out into the world and find yourself a new and healthy relationship.

如何像治疗骨折一样治愈失恋

（文◎F.戴安娜·巴斯）

首先，失恋之人得意识到他是“真的受伤了”。根据医生的推荐，以下6个步骤能助你从身体伤害中恢复。

1. 给自己充分的治愈时间。多休息，吃好喝好，哪怕你没什么胃口。食物能滋养身体，而处于失恋痛苦中的人体需要足够的营养来自我修复。

当身体受伤时，你通常被告知在未来一段时期内不要去触碰伤口。根据梅奥医学中心的研究，在大脑受伤（比如脑震荡）之后，过度用脑和过早恢复体力活动都会令病情加重，并且有可能让病人受到永久性的损害。分手之痛也是如此。有时情伤的痛苦似乎不能完全被人所理解。当某人身体受伤时，比如打石膏、拄拐杖等，通常会得到很多同情。对失恋的人，人们会稍微表示一下同情，但通常会希望他们尽快振作起来，尽管情伤的治愈根本没那么快。在这种情况下，你得提醒自己，或许也礼貌地提醒你好心的亲朋好友，治愈情伤跟身体上的伤一样需要时间，这一点非常重要。

2. 在分手之后做什么类似于身体受伤后的复健？马上开始新的约会？并不尽然。分手之后马上开始新的约会，无异于摔断腿6周之后就开始跑5英里（约8千米）。治愈情伤就跟复健一样，应徐徐图之，给你的身体和精神以习惯的空间。身体受伤后，你得重建身体肌肉，情感受伤后，你也一样得重建情感肌肉。你得慢慢来，或许从跟朋友一起度过一个安静的夜晚、一起去喝一杯开始。你自己能体会参加这些活动的感受，当你觉得自己准备好了，就可以尝试规模更大的社交活动了。

3. 当你重新开始约会后，得对一些焦虑和不适感做好准备。在这些情况下自我防备很自然，你会不自觉地对可能再次受伤产生恐惧。放慢步伐、保持轻松能助你克服恐惧，就好像身体受伤后的复健活动中，你会循序渐进地增加运动量一样。

我会建议我的顾客跟他们的约会对象坦白最近刚分手。尽管现在一些咨询师对此并不赞同，但我认为这样做能为他们提供更多空间，让他们慢慢来。这就好像你刚拿掉腿上的石膏，不能马上下地跑步，但并不意味着你在近期内都无法跑步。当然，跟约会对象坦白刚刚分手很可能把他们吓跑，但我感觉会被吓跑的那些人也并非你在这段非常时期中的最佳约会对象。

4. 在某些时刻，你会察觉自己真的好多了。这个阶段的危险之一是，你可能已经非常适应这种失恋疗伤状态了。你也许会害怕新的尝试；你也许不仅仅得到了真正需要的失恋后的正能量，还得到了人生的正能量；你也许已经习惯了自怜自艾或怨恨前任。当你实际上已经准备好跟旧感情告别时，如果有了这些想法和感觉，就很可能裹足不前。你是否害怕重蹈覆辙？是否准备好了在未来的约会、恋爱中做出一些改变？利用这段过渡期来衡量你对恋爱真实的期待和欲望，这也是你客观总结上一段失败感情教训的好时机。你是不是忽视了一些问题的早期迹象？你能否在面对困难时承担起自己的责任？下一次你怎样才能做得更好？对未来的伴侣你有什么样的未能在上一段关系中实现的期待？

5. 一旦走出情伤后，就不要再执着于已结束的感情。虽然你已准备好迎接新的感情，但很有可能不会立刻遇到新的心仪对象。利用这个机会去结识更多的人，那些要不是失恋你可能永远不会认识的人。学习新的东西，同时也别忘记旧的爱好。别一时冲动做决定，也别因为某些事让你感觉舒服、新鲜就立刻拥抱它。

6. 最后，请记住伤痛会带来成长和新的方向。用再次复原的心去感受这个世界，去寻找一段完善的新感情。

Love Me Still but Know Not Why

（文◎ John Willbye）

Love not me for comely grace,
For my pleasing eye or face,
Nor for any outward part,
No, nor for a constant heart;
For these may fail or turn to ill,
So thou and I shall sever;
Keep, therefore, a true woman's eye,
And love me still but know not why
So hast thou the same reason still
To doat upon me ever!

像不知道原因那样爱我

（文◎约翰·威尔比）

我的爱人
请不要
为了我秀美的气质而爱我
不要为了我动人的眼眸，或者悦目的面庞，而爱我
也不要为了我外貌上的其他什么，而爱我
甚至，也不要因为彼此忠贞的心，而爱着我
因为这一些爱我的原因啊
它们终会失色， 或者不再奏效
而到那时
你便将
与我分离
所以，我的爱人啊
且把你那真挚的眼神留住
不知道是为了什么地
那么爱着我
那样的话
你就可以永远地
深爱着我
为了亘古不变的理由

I Like the Subtle Feeling
我喜欢这样淡淡的感觉

（文© Anonymous 佚名）

I like the subtle fresh green budding from the branches of the tree—the herald of spring, ushering in the dawn...

I like the subtle flow of cloud that makes the sky seem even more vast, azure and immense...

I like the subtle wind. In spring, it steals a kiss on my cheek; in autumn, it caresses my face; in summer, it brings in cool sweet smell; in winter, it carries a crisp chilliness...

I like the subtle taste of tea that last long after a sip. The subtle bitter is what it is meant to be...

I like the subtle friendship that does not hold people together. In stead, an occasional greeting spreads our longings far beyond...

I like the subtle longing for a friend, when I sink deeply in a couch, mind wandering in memories of the past...

Love should also be subtle, without enslaving the ones fallen into her arms. Not a bit less nor a bit more...

我喜欢看树枝上那淡淡的嫩绿，它是春天的使者，它是一天清晨的开始……

我喜欢天空中那淡淡的云，它将天空衬得更高更蓝更宽……

我喜欢淡淡的风。春风轻吻脸颊，秋风拂面温柔，夏天的风送来凉爽，冬天的风带来清凉……

我喜欢喝淡淡的茶，淡淡之中才能品出它余味的清香，淡淡的苦才是它原来的味道……

我喜欢追求淡淡的友谊。彼此之间不需要天天在一起，偶尔一句：你好吗？思念就像发芽一样蔓延开来……

我喜欢淡淡地思念一个人，静静地将自己包围在沙发之中，任思绪在回忆里飘荡……

爱也要淡淡的。爱，不要成为囚，少是愁多也是忧……

Walk Beside Me. Just Be My Friend

走在我旁边，做我的朋友就好

（文◎ Anonymous 佚名）

Friendship... is born at the moment when one man says to another "What! You too? I thought that no one but myself ..."

— C.S. Lewis, *The Four Loves*

当一个人对另一个人说“什么？你也这样？我以为只有我一个人这样呢……”的时候，友谊就诞生了。

——英国著名学者、文学家 C.S. 刘易斯《四种爱》

Don't walk in front of me... I may not follow.

Don't walk behind me... I may not lead.

Walk beside me... just be my friend.

— Albert Camus

不要走在我前面，我可能追不上你。

不要走在我后面，我可能不会引路。

走在我旁边，做我的朋友就好。

——法国作家阿尔贝 · 加缪

A friend is someone who knows all about you and still loves you.

— Elbert Hubbard

朋友就是知道你的一切，但依然爱你的人。

——美国作家阿尔伯特 · 哈伯德

Good friends, good books, and a sleepy conscience: this is the ideal life.

— Mark Twain

拥有良书、益友和一颗宁静的心：这就是理想的生活。

——美国作家马克·吐温

The truth is, everyone is going to hurt you. You just got to find the ones worth suffering for.

— Bob Marley

事实是，每个人都会伤害你。你只需找到那些值得让你忍受伤害的人。

——牙买加唱作歌手、雷鬼乐鼻祖鲍勃·马利

There is nothing I would not do for those who are really my friends. I have no notion of loving people by halves, it is not my nature.

— Jane Austen, *Northanger Abbey*

我愿意为我那些真正的朋友做任何事。我不会只付出一半的爱，那不是我。

——简·奥斯汀《诺桑觉寺》

When someone loves you, the way they talk about you is different. You feel safe and comfortable.

— Jess C. Scott, *The Intern*

别人爱你的时候，他们谈论你的方式是不一样的。你会觉得安全、舒服。

——杰斯·C. 斯科特《实习生》

There is nothing better than a friend, unless it is a friend with chocolate.

— Linda Grayson

没有什么比一个朋友更棒，除非那个朋友还带着巧克力。

——演员琳达·格雷森

Life is an awful, ugly place to not have a best friend.

— Sarah Dessen, *Someone Like You*

没有好朋友，生活就是一个糟糕的、丑陋的地方。

——萨拉·迪森《像你一样的人》

What is a friend? A single soul dwelling in two bodies.

— Aristotle

朋友是什么？同时住在两个身体里的同一个灵魂。

——亚里士多德

Love Is Enough

（文◎ Willian Morris）

Love is enough: though the world be a-waning,
And the woods have no voice but the voice of complaining,
Though the skies be too dark for dim eyes to discover
The gold-cups and daisies fair blooming thereunder,
Though the hills be held shadows, and the sea a dark wonder,
And this day draw a veil over all deeds passed over,
Yet their hands shall not tremble, their feet shall not falter:
The void shall not weary, the fear shall not alter
These lips and these eyes of the loved and the lover.

爱就足够了

（文◎威廉·莫里斯）

爱就足够了
纵使生活像一轮渐渐亏缺的月亮
纵使树林里传来的除了埋怨没有其他声响
纵使天那么昏沉而眼神已经黯淡
再也看不清田野里金盏花与白色百合盛开的烂漫
纵使山谷中魅影重重，大海黑得像团迷雾
纵使每天经过的一切，像被一块面纱蒙住
爱人啊，他们的手不会颤抖，他们的步子不会蹒跚
空虚或是畏惧，都不会蹉跎不会改变
爱与被爱的人儿
眼里的光芒
唇上的芬芳。绘英语

第5章

成长路上，全新的冒险

New Adventure

(文◎ Ascharff)

When I jumped into the present I landed at a train station, ready to take on a new adventure.

I felt like a sad puppy, Niagara falls rushing from my eyes. Until, I found the hiding place where rain shivers on top of the big blooming petals of a flower. I turned hope on high and saw the bright yellow sun peaking through the big grey clouds. He was the enemy of green hiding within the rough, rugged branches of an old willow tree. He wasn't tender, he's the opposite, strong, like a big sumo wrestler taking a stand to fight. I tossed my sadness into the wind, and it returned a soothing surprise.

全新的冒险

（文◎阿沙尔夫 译◎ Kane）

当我回过神来，已经在一个火车站里，准备踏上全新的冒险之旅。

但我站在飞流直下的尼亚加拉大瀑布前时，却觉察到自己的渺小，像一只悲伤的小犬。直到我发现那个隐秘的地方，藏着一株坚挺的花，雨滴重重地落在它的花瓣上。我抬眼望向远方，金黄色的阳光穿透了厚厚的灰色云层。粗糙的树干里的绿色苔藓，太阳的光亮是它们的大敌。但太阳并不总像春天那样温柔，恰恰相反，他很强大，像一个大块头的相扑者，扎好马步准备战斗。想到这里，我将那无谓的悲伤丢进风里，风声回馈我以宽慰。

I Wish You Enough

（文◎ Anonymous ）

At the airport, I overheard a father and daughter in their last moments together. Her flight was ready for boarding. Standing near the departure gate. They hugged and he said, "I love you, I wish you enough." She in turn said, "Daddy, our life together has been more than enough. Your love is all I ever needed. I wish you enough, too, Daddy."

They kissed goodbye and she left. The man walked over towards the window near where I was seated. I could see that he wanted and needed to cry.

I tried not to intrude upon his privacy, but he welcomed me by asking, "Have you ever said goodbye to someone knowing that it would be forever?"

"Yes, I have." Saying that brought back memories I had of expressing my love and appreciation for all that my Dad had done for me. Recognizing that his days were numbered, I took the time to tell him, face to face, how much he meant to me. So I knew what this man was going through.

"Forgive me for asking, but why is this goodbye

forever?" I asked.

"I am old and she lives much too far away. I have challenges ahead and the reality is, her next trip back will be for my funeral." he said.

"I heard you say 'I wish you enough' May I ask what that means?"

He began to smile. "That is a wish that has been handed down through the generations. My parents used to say it to everyone."

The man paused a moment, then looked up, as if trying to remember the details.

"When we say I wish you enough, we want the other persons to have a life filled with enough good things to sustain them."

He then turned to me and shared the following, as if he were reciting it from memory:

I wish you enough sun to keep your attitude bright.

I wish you enough rain to appreciate the sun more.

I wish you enough happiness to keep your spirits up.

I wish you enough pain so that the smallest joys in life appear much bigger.

I wish you enough gain to satisfy your wanting.

I wish you enough loss to appreciate all that you possess.

I wish you enough hellos to get you through the final Goodbye.

Then the man began to sob and walked away.

愿你尽享人生

（文◎佚名）

在机场我无意中听到父女俩在最后分别时刻的谈话。女儿正准备上飞机，他们站在机舱门附近。他们拥抱着，父亲说："我爱你，我希望你能知足常乐，尽享人生。"女儿回答说："爸爸，我们在一起生活了这么长时间，我已经很知足了，您给我的爱也够了，我也希望您能知足常乐，尽享人生，爸爸！"

吻别后，女儿走了。父亲朝着我座位附近的窗子走过来，我可以看出他忍不住要哭。

我尽力不触及他的隐私，但他却向我打招呼，问："你曾经有过明知是永别却还对某人说再见的经历吗？"

"我有过这种经历。"这句话让我想起我父亲曾为我所做的一切，向他表示过我的爱和感激。知道他在世的日子不多后，我特意当面对他说他对我有多么重要。所以我理解这个人此时

的感受。

“请原谅我问一句，为什么是永别呢？”我问。

“我老了，她又住得那么远。我的未来生活充满挑战。实际上，她再回来的时候便是参加我的葬礼了。”他说。

“我听到你说‘我希望你知足常乐，尽享人生’，那是什么意思？”

他露出微笑：“那个愿望是我们家代代相传的。我的父母过去常对每个人说。”

那个人顿了一下，抬了抬头，像是在尽力回想其中的细节。

“我们对人们说知足常乐，尽享人生，就是希望对方的生活里充满幸事，支撑他们走下去。”

他转向我，对我说了下面这些话，像是在背诵：

我希望你有足够的阳光让你乐观。

我希望你有足够的雨水让你更加感激阳光。

我希望你有足够的幸福使你情绪激昂。

我希望你有足够的痛苦感受生命中微小的欢乐带来的幸福。

我希望你得到更多，满足你的需要。

我希望你失去更多，珍惜所有。

我希望你在永别后能广交朋友。

那个人开始抽泣，然后走开了。

Brave Will Be by Your Side

勇气伴你前行

（文◎ Anonymous 佚名）

When it all feels like
everything's impossible,
And you don't fit right in a
crowd,
Go wild and break the mold.
If you don't try you'll never fly,
But you gotta be brave, yeah.
Say you're out of luck,
Knocked down in the dust.
You've got a fragile heart.
I know, cause so do I, yeah.
Stuck here strugglin',
Harder to believe that.
Things may fall apart,
You can't give up the fight, yeah.

Sometimes, running on low,
Takes you all the way home.
Prove how far you can go,
You've gotta show the world.
(Refrain)
You gotta be brave, yeah.
There is a remedy,
Patched up easily.
Learn to love yourself,
And never hide the scars.
There's been damage done.
But the battle's won.
You were strong enough,
To get to where you are, yeah.
(Refrain)
(Refrain)
You gotta be brave, yeah.
Oooooh, ooooh,
You can stand tall,
You can stay strong,
You can show everyone.
Oooooh, ooooh,
You were your own,
Let'em all know,
That you can be brave.
(Refrain)
(Refrain)
You gotta be brave, yeah.

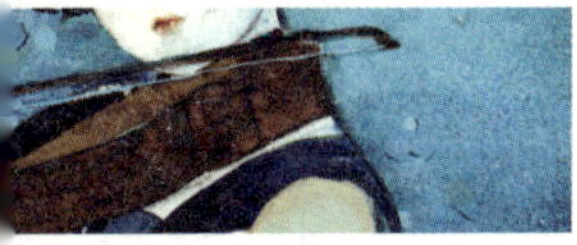

日本作家龙之湖太郎曾在其作品《问题儿童都来自异世界》中这样写道：“就算因为恐惧而害怕得浑身颤抖，却依然向前迈出一步，这便是勇气。”我们在婴儿期学步时一次次摔倒又一次次站起来，直到双腿越来越健壮。最终学会了走路，学会了奔跑。一如学步，我们直面恐惧时，也会从每一次和它的较量中获得力量、勇气和信心。

Brave《勇气》这首歌出自美国乐队 Action Item 于 2013 年 1 月 1 日发行的专辑，这张专辑中的歌曲热情洋溢、曲调优美，散发着浓浓的青春气息。有乐迷评论说，自己在最艰难的时候一直循环播放着这首充满正能量的歌曲，提醒自己要坚强起来，不到最后一刻决不放弃。这首歌的曲风偏轻摇滚，旋律流畅而清新，富有层次感的鼓点和主唱 Brian Cag 的声音结合得恰到好处，听起来振奋人心。

一如歌词所唱的，如果你不尝试，你就永远无法展翅高飞。群鸿戏海，野鹤游天，如果想要去广阔的天地欣赏波澜壮阔的景色，首先要有一颗不畏困难、勇敢前行的心。勇气就像是藏于胸中的一把锋芒四射的利剑，它能砍断黑暗之路上的荆棘藤蔓，引领意志坚强之人不断突破自我，实现最初的梦想。

第一小节第二句歌词中的一个小词 fit，它在这里作动词，意为“适应”，这句歌词的意思就是“而你觉得自己在一群人当中格格不入”。有一个与此相关的词组为 fit in(with sb. / sth.)，它的意思是“（与某人）相处融洽，合得来，适应（某个环境）”。比如你在学校跟同学们相处得很好，你就可以说：“Fit in well with my classmates at school. ”fit 作动词时，还可以指“和……相称；符合”。中国歌手

邓紫棋与韩国“长腿欧巴”金秀贤一起为德芙巧克力拍摄了一则广告，其中有一句台词为“听说，下雨天巧克力和音乐更配哦”。我们就可以将它翻译成 It is said that chocolate and music fit better on rainy days. 再来看第三句歌词中的词组 go wild，它的意思是“变得非常激动”，比如我们可以说 go wild with joy（欣喜若狂）。紧随其后的还有一个词组 break the mold，它是什么意思呢？ Mold 这个单词的本义是“模子、模具”，这里指的是那些束缚我们的东西，即“模式”，所以这个词组的意思就是“打破模式；打破陈规”，比如：The future belongs to those who break the mold（未来属于那些打破陈规的人）。

第二小节中有一个短语 fall apart，它的本义是“破碎、断裂”，比如：The chair fell apart when I sat on it. 在这里它指的是“（组织、制度、关系等）崩溃，破裂”，比如你的朋友尚未做好准备就想匆匆行动，你就可以告诉他：“Get fully prepared, or your plan will fall apart.（做好充分的准备吧。不然你的计划就会失败）”。

再来看第五小节，第一句歌词中有一个单词 remedy，它的本义是“药品；疗法”，cold remedy（感冒药）、cough remedy（咳嗽药）、herbal remedy（草药）、folk remedy（民间药方）。在这首歌中，它指的是“补救办法；改进措施”，比如当我们想表达某个问题有许多解决办法时，就可以表达成：There are a number of possible remedies to this problem. 大家对第二句歌词中 patch up 这个词组

可能会有点儿陌生，它的本义是“修补；草草修理”，比如你的外套破了，你就可以跟妈妈说：“Mom, could you please help me patch up my coat?”在这首歌中，它指的是“仓促（或粗糙地）做成；拼凑成”，比如palch up an agreement（草草达成一项协议）。这个词组也可以指“临时包扎；快速处理（伤口）”，当你看到有小朋友因踢球而受伤时，就可以安慰他说：“The doctor will soon patch you up.（大夫很快就会给你把伤口包扎好的。）”

人生漫漫，谁都会有失意之时。不管你遇到多大的挫折，遭到多大的打击，请你一定要努力忘记过去的伤痛，勇敢前行。因为如果你不尝试。你就永远无法展翅高飞。

Don't Allow "But" to Kill Your Dream

(文◎ Anonymous)

Most of us, go through life pretending, that we don't have any special goals or ambitions or desires, when really down inside we do really want more.

We block ourselves, and we use this words almost like we where in a trans.

Like we sleepwalking through life. That we find ways to cancel our dreams.

A lot of things we want do a lot of places. we would like to go a lot of things we would like to experience.

And we just stop at "but"..."But" will cause you to hide out behind fear. "But" will cause you to come out with all type of excuses that you can validate your in action and not acting on your dream.

"But" is a dream killer. But most people, you know what they do? Most people go through life quietly and safely tiptoeing to the early grave.

We've been holding back, we have ideas that we don't act on. Things we want do, we afraid to take a chances.

See a lot of people say "No" to things that they don't even know what they are saying "No" to.

Don't allow "but" to keep you in the corner.

别让“但是”扼杀你的梦想

（文◎佚名）

我们大多数人一辈子都在假装，假装自己没有什么追求和野心。而在我们的内心深处，谁不想得到更多呢？

可是我们会刻意地不去想这些，因为觉得梦想与现实相去甚远。

然后行尸走肉一般过此一生。不知不觉间泯灭所有念想。

很多我们想做的事情，许多我们想去的地方，很多我们想拥有的经历和体验，我们都会在“但是”面前打消念头。“但是”只会让我们逃离恐惧，“但是”只会让你编造各种借口，让你不去行动，不去追求你的梦想。

“但是”足以扼杀人的梦想。你知道大多数人是怎么做的吗？他们一辈子过得安逸平常，悄无声息地过早死去。

我们都被消磨了志气，空有想法却不付诸行动。

想做事情，却又不敢冒风险，大多数人习惯了拒绝，虽然他们都不知道自己拒绝的是什么。

不要因为“但是”让你缚手缚脚。

I Might as Well Tell You, I'm Lonely

（文◎ Adrienne Rich）

You're wondering if I'm lonely:
OK then, yes, I'm lonely
as a plane rides lonely and level
on its radio beam, aiming
across the Rockies
for the blue-strung aisles
of an airfield on the ocean.

If I'm lonely
it must be the loneliness
of waking first, of breathing
dawns' first cold breath on the city
of being the one awake
in a house wrapped in sleep

If I'm lonely
it's with the rowboat ice-fast on the shore
in the last red light of the year
that knows what it is, that knows it's neither
ice nor mud nor winter light
but wood, with a gift for burning

不妨告诉你，我是孤独的

（文 ◎艾德丽安 · 里奇　译 ◎ 李文俊）

你在寻思我是不是孤独：
是的，不妨告诉你，我是孤独的
像一架依靠定向无线电波
在孤独地飞行和掌握高度的飞机
要翻越落基山脉去寻求
那条被漫天蓝色挤成珠链似的跑道

如果说我孤独
那必定是那种孤独：
第一个醒来，呼吸到全城
破晓时分第一口寒冽的空气
第一个醒来，当全屋子的人
都蒙着头在昏昏沉沉地酣睡

如果说我孤独
那也是一条冻结在岸上的小船
映照着岁暮的最后一抹红霞
它知道自己是什么，知道自己
既不是冰，也不是泥和冬天的寒光
而是木头，生来能炽烈地燃烧。

绘英语

Change Destiny
改写命运

（文◎ Anonymous 佚名）

Every second, we have the opportunity to make the next second greater than now.

Because destiny isn't a matter of chance. It's a matter of choice.

So let go of what others want you to be.

Change is in all of us.

And the only person your destiny to become, is the person you decide to be.

Change destiny.

每一秒，我们都有机会让下一秒变得比现在更好。

因为真正决定命运的不是运气，而是选择。

所以，放下世俗中别人对你的期望。

改变在于我们的内心。

所以你的命运在于你选择成为什么样的人。

改写命运。绘英语

Meet The Episode of Fate with Resignation

（文◎ Anonymous ）

I said to my mind, "Show me your anger now." One by one, my life's every incident of anger rose and made itself known. Every injustice, every betrayal, every loss, every rage. I saw them all, one by one, and I acknowledged their existence. I felt each piece of anger completely, as if it were happening for the first time, and then I would say, "Come into my heart now. You can rest there. It's safe now. It's over. I love you." This went on for hours, and I swung between these mighty poles of opposite feelings—experiencing the anger thoroughly for one bone-rattling moment, and then experiencing a total coolness, as the anger entered my heart as if through a door, laid itself down, curled up against its brothers and gave up fighting.

Then came the most difficult part. "Show me your shame." I asked my mind. Dear God, the horrors that I saw then. A pitiful parade of all my failings, my lies, my selfishness, jealousy, arrogance. I didn't blink from any of it, though. "Show me your worst." I said. When I tried to invite these units of shame into my heart, they each hesitated at the door, saying, "No—you don't want me in there... don't you know what I did?" and I would say, "I do want you. Even you. I do. Even you are welcome here. It's OK. You are forgiven. You are part of me. You can rest now. It's over."

When all this was finished, I was empty. Nothing was fighting in my mind anymore. I looked into my heart, at my own goodness, and I saw its capacity. I saw that my heart was not even nearly full, not even after having taken in and tended to all those calamitous urchins of sorrow and anger and shame; my heart could easily have received and forgiven even more. Its love was infinite.

接受生命中每一段插曲吧

（文◎佚名）

我对自己的心说："现在让我看看你的愤怒。"而后，我生命中的每一段愤怒插曲一一出现，介绍自己。每一个误解，每一个背叛，每一个失落，每一次愤怒。我一一看见它们，对它们的存在表示认可。我彻底感受每一次愤怒，仿佛头一遭发生，然后我说："现在进入我的心来吧。你可以在此歇息。现在安全了，都过去了。我爱你。"如此持续数个小时，我在这些对立的感受之间摇来荡去——前一刻彻底体验震撼人心的愤怒，下一刻却又在愤怒走进我的心门，躺下来，舒服地蜷伏在兄弟身边，停止争斗之时，体验到完全的冷静。

接着，最困难的部分到来了。"让我看看你羞愧的事。"我向我的心提出要求。天哪，随后我看见这些令人惧怕的事。我卑贱的失败、谎言、自私、嫉妒、傲慢一一展现出来。然而我并未逃避。"让我看看你最糟的部分。"当我把这些羞愧部分请入我的心，它们各个都在门口犹豫起来，说："不——你不要让我进去吧……你难道不明白我做了什么？"我说："我真的要你。即使是你，真的，甚至连你也欢迎来到这里。没事了。你得到原谅。你是我的一部分。现在你可以歇息，都过去了。"

这一切都结束之后，我已成空。我心中不再有任何争斗。我探查自己的心，审查自己的美德，我看见内心的容量。我看见我的心甚至尚未饱和，甚至在收容那些不幸的哀伤、愤怒与羞愧之后，我的心可以轻而易举地接受更多，宽容更多。它的爱无穷无尽。绘英语

If You Don't Walk Out, You Will Think that This Is the Whole World

如果不出去走走，你会认为这就是整个世界

（文◎ Anonymous 佚名）

《天堂电影院》中老头子与多多之间的对话

Alfredo: Living here day after day, you think it's the center of the world believe nothing will ever change, then you leave, a year, two years, when you come back, everything's changed, the thread's broken, what you came to find isn't there, what was yours is gone, you have to go away for a while, make something of your life before you come back to your place, to the land where you were born. But now, no . It is not possible. Right now you're blinder than I am.

Salvatore: Who said that? Gary Cooper? James Stewart? Henry Fonda? Eh?

Alfredo: No, Toto. Nobody said it. This time it's all me. Life isn't like in the movies. Life...is much harder. If you don't walk out, you will think that this is the whole world.

阿尔夫莱多：在这里居住了一天又一天，你认为这里就是世界的中心。你相信一切都永不会改变。然后你离开了，一年，两年，当你回来时，一切都变了。那条线断了，你所寻找的并不是这里。你只能再次离开很长时间……很多年……直到你能回来寻找你的家人，你出生的土地。但是现在不可能。现在你比我还要瞎。

萨尔瓦多：这些是谁说的？加里·库帕？詹姆士·斯图尔特？亨利·福达？嗯？

阿尔夫莱多：不是，多多，没有人说过。这次是我自己说的。生活并不像电影，生活……更艰难。如果你不出去走走，你就会以为这就是全世界。

What Is the Meaning of Travelling Alone

(文◎ Anonymous)

Missed flights, cancelled rides and changed plans make solo travelers incredibly resilient. After grappling through the ups and downs of a solo trip, you're capable of bouncing back from pretty much anything life throws your way.

Solo adventure taught me a ton about relationships and human connection. Solo traveling pushed me out of my comfort zone.

Yes, safety is a concern in certain locations, and it's often pleasant to have someone to share the scenery with. But never underestimate the glory of traveling solo, because you'll learn things you can't learn any other way.

If you have the heart of an explorer, traveling alone is an excellent way to see the world on your own terms. But it can also be scary, particularly if you're a woman concerned about her safety on a solo

trip to far-flung corners of the globe. Self-reliance was at the core of your being.

As we "grow up" it becomes impractical to up-and-leave. Valid reasons like job security, relationships and making rent replace our once happy-to-rough-it-for-months mentality.

As a solo traveler, you are more open, more willing to make friends, and share experiences with others along the way, and this reveals itself in your actions and your face.

The ironic thing about traveling solo is that you're rarely ever actually alone. There's always an open seat next to you, whether you're on a plane, train, or bus, and sometimes that can lead to unwanted advances.

一个人旅行的意义在哪里

（文◎佚名）

飞机误点、行程取消还有计划改变，独自旅行者因而变得异常平静，接受各种变化。经历过独自旅行的起起伏伏，无论人生途中有何坎坷，都可以自我恢复。

一个人旅行教会了我很多有关人际关系的处理，促使我走出自己的舒适区。

确实，有些地方的安全问题是要考虑的，同他人共享美景往往也令人愉悦。但不要低估独自旅行的荣光，因为你能学到别处学不到的东西。

但如果你内心是个探险家，那么一个人旅行是看这个世界绝佳的方法。独自一人也可能很骇人，尤其你若是一个女孩子，独自一人去世界遥远的角落不免担心安全问题。依靠自己是你存在的核心。

我们慢慢“长大”，“说走就走”变得越来越不可行。工作安全感、人际关系和房屋租金等真切存在的理由替代了我们曾经“快乐度日、得过且过”的思维方式。

一个人旅行，你会变得更开明，更愿意结交朋友，更乐于和别人分享一路的游历体验，这会体现在你的行为中，也会写在你的脸上。

具讽刺意味的是，独自旅行时你很少真正独处。你身旁总会有一个空位，无论你在飞机、火车还是公交车上，有时还会带你开启一场你不曾期待的冒险。

Living in the Moment

（文◎ Anonymous ）

The first day of my junior year, I feel boring about everything. Teachers talked endlessly, children made fun of each other, it can't be more boring. And I had not finished my homework till dinner. The sun had just gone down and the sky was so clear and the stars seemed so big that I got tempted into going to the beach for a while.

I walked along the small wooden bridge that weaved its way through a thicket of trees. The lamps that bordered the outside lit everything just enough so I could see where I was going. I didn't bother to bring anything. I didn't feel like thinking. All I really wanted to do was relax.

I walked for a few minutes before the trees around me began to disappear and the wood under my feet gradually turned into sand. The sounds of the ocean began to make itself apparent and before I knew it the trees were gone. Nothing but the open sea was in front of me. The stars filled the sky from horizon to horizon, and a small crescent moon was randomly placed in the middle of it all.

I slipped off my sandals and felt the cool sand on the bottoms of my feet. It was quiet and peaceful, not soul around. Only the sounds of the crashing waves could be heard and the stars were shining. I felt I can see far, I tried hard to feel the beauty of nothing, but I failed. I saw the things familiar, my friends, my family, and I want them to be here with me to enjoy the nature. I love this moment for sudden and I am living in the moment.

生活就在这一刻

（文◎佚名）

上中学的第一天，我就觉得自己厌倦了这一切，老师在讲台上无休止地讲着，同学互相扯皮，无聊透顶。而且，晚餐的时候我还没做完功课。太阳刚刚落下，天空如此晴朗，把那星星的轮廓都放大了，我突然想到海边走走。

我沿着逶迤的木栈桥在林中前行，一点点微弱的灯光刚好能照见眼前的路。我什么都没带，什么都不去想，只想休息。

我在树林中走了几分钟，树木逐渐变得稀疏，而脚下也渐渐有了沙地的质感。树木在身边消失，海浪声随之而来。我的前方，蓦地现出一片宽阔的海。星光填补了夜空，把地平线的一端到另一端填满了，一枚小小的新月随意地挂在中间。

我脱掉了凉鞋，赤脚去感受沙子的凉意。静谧，而又平和的海边，空无一人。只有波浪冲刷着，星光闪耀着。我觉得我能看到很远的地方，我希望能够感受这空无之美。但我失败了。我能看见的是我熟悉的一切，我的朋友，我的家人，我希望能和他们同享这自然之美。我突然间爱上了这一刻，生活就在这一刻。

Together

（文◎ Omar Merza ）

Years ago, after being put in bed to sleep, a child stared up at the glowing stars on the ceiling of the room. There would be no sleep for the child. Her brain was too busy imagining all the possibilities the world had to offer. She could not keep track of her thoughts; she would think of the absolute perfect scenario only for her mind to wander off to a better place moments later.

"I want to be a black belt pilot cook."

"I'll be the first mermaid writer president ever."

Wishes were made to stars on ceilings, stars made real by the sheer power of imagination. Finally, the child fell asleep and journeyed into a world where scenarios that were even more impossible became reality.

Then you woke up. I woke up.

We wake up to reality.

There is a sudden and frightening realization. You are not that child anymore. You are what people consider to be a grown up. You have a job, but there is only one problem. You hate it. That's fine because you can still go out with your friends and have a great time, but it's in crowds where you feel most alone now. Well at least you have your writing, dancing, drawing, training, sculpting...Oh wait, you stopped doing that too. There will always be your family, but you sadly no longer have anything to talk to them about.

Days pass through your fingers like grains of sand. Life becomes a chore.

Yeah it could be worse, much worse, but what hurts is that it could also be better, so much better.

You are now on auto-pilot; surviving, not living. You feel paralyzed. Everyday you say tomorrow will be different. Tomorrow comes and nothing happens. Countless false dawns later you try to numb yourself and accept the fact that this is life. Not many people you know are truly happy, so why should you be?

Still, the nagging sensation does not disappear. That feeling that something isn't right, that something is missing persists. There is an emptiness. You try to find distractions to keep you from facing it. You try desperately to have great weekends, you "fall in love" ridiculously easily, pick up new hobbies only to drop them as quickly as you picked them up, and watch endless Ted Talks. You attempt to convince yourself that you are trying, that you are changing. But you are not.

This is not what you expected. The funny thing with expectations is that they are usually the furthest thing from reality. I know mine are, and that proves to be extremely difficult to deal with. This is not where you thought you would be. This is not the life you were supposed to lead.

If you have ever felt this way before, or are feeling this way now, then rest assured that it is only proof that you are human. Everyone gets these feelings from time to time. We all feel lost, alone, empty, restless, impatient, or incompetent at one point or another.

Everyone is struggling. Everyone feels pain. There is absolutely no shame in that. People just have different ways of showing it or dealing with it. Look around you when you walk down the street, look around you when you are with your friends, family, or in the office. Look at the people's faces. They all have their own worries, fears, pain, hopes, and dreams.

We all suffer.

It may sound a bit selfish, but it is a relief to know that you are not the only one going through this. I am with you.

And I am here to remind you of what you already know but have chosen to bury deep inside of yourself, what I myself at times have tried to forget.

That there must be more to all of this. That this cannot be what life is about. The world will never be perfect, but there is magic out there. There is adventure to be had. There is true happiness to be found.

I feel this now just as I felt it when I was a child wishing upon a star.

Never forget that every single atom in your body was formed in the core of a star billions of years go.

There is a universe, inside of you and out, waiting to be discovered.

It won't be easy, this journey. Nothing of substantial worth has ever come easily.

Take my hand.

Feel it tremble.

I am just as terrified as you.

You are not alone.

Yes you have your own path and I have mine, but luckily, at least for this moment, our paths intertwine.

Breath in deeply and put your foot out in front of you. Take that first step forward.

We can do it.

Together.

我们一起前行

（文◎奥马尔·梅尔察）

多年前，有一个孩子躺在床上，她没有睡觉，而是盯着房间天花板上发亮的星星看。她的脑海里想象着所有世界上可能发生的事。她自己都无法跟上自己的思路，这一刻，她想象一个相当完美的情景。片刻之后，她就走神了，想到了另一个更加美好的情景。

“我想成为一名高级厨师向导。”

“我会成为第一个身为美人鱼的作家。”

她向着天花板上的星星许着愿望，因为孩子的想象力，星星也好像变得真实了。最后，孩子睡着了，进入一个更不可能成为现实的世界中去了。

然后你醒了，我也醒了。

我们在现实中醒来。

这种领悟既突然又可怕。你不是那个孩子了。在其他人眼里，你是大人了。你有一份工作，但你却厌恶这份工作。这没什么，因为你仍然可以和你的朋友一起玩。但是即使在人群中，现在你也会感觉很孤独。至少你还可以写作、跳舞、画画、训练、雕刻……等一下！对了，你已经不再做这些了。你的家人还在，但可悲的是，你和他们也没什么好谈的了。

时间像细沙在你的指缝间流逝。生活里全是零零碎碎的事。生活可以变得很糟，或是更糟。但让人伤感的是，生活也可以变得很好，或是更好。

你现在就像是在自动驾驶的状态下，

为了活下去，而不是为了活得有意义。你的感觉变得麻木。你每天都说，明天会不同。但真当明天到来，却什么都没有发生。在经历无数的虚幻曙光之后，你想麻木自己接受这个事实——这就是生活。你知道没有多少人是真正幸福的，那为什么你就应该幸福呢?

不过，令人不安的感觉不会消失。你感觉好像什么地方有些不对，总觉得少点儿什么。这就是一种空虚的感觉。你尽量不分心去想它，不去面对这个问题。你尽最大的努力尝试过好周末，你很轻易地坠入爱河，培养新的爱好，只是为了让你一想起这些问题，就能把它们丢到脑后，然后看无尽的 TED（TED 是美国的一家私有非营利机构，该机构以它组织的 TED 大会著称，这个会议的宗旨是“值得传播的创意”。）演讲视频。你试图说服自己，自己正在做不同的尝试、正在改变。但事实上你没有。

这不是你所期待的。有趣的是，预期所想的事，通常会与现实相差甚远。我知道我自己就是这样的，这个问题还很难处理。这不是你想过的生活。这不是你应该过的生活。

如果你以前有过这样的感觉，或者现在就有这种感觉。那么请放心，这只证明你是一个人而已。每个人都会时不时有这些感觉。我们都会或多或少感到迷失、孤独、空虚、不安、焦躁或是无能。

每个人都在挣扎。每个人都会感到疼痛。不必对此感到羞愧。只是人们会有不同的表现和处理方式而已。当你走在街上时，环顾四周的人是什么样的。当你和家人、朋友在一起或是在办公室里的时候，看看周围的人是什么样的。看看他们的脸。他们也都有自己的焦虑、恐惧、痛苦、希望和梦想。

我们都遭受着苦难。

这听起来似乎有些自私。但当你知道不止自己在经历这种事情时，你还是会感觉到一丝欣慰。

我会一直陪伴着你。

我会提醒你，那些你已经知道的，但是决定深埋内心的事，那些有时自己都试图忘记的事。

除此之外，还有更多的东西。生活不可能只包含这种感觉。世界永远都不会是完美的，但还是会有奇迹，会有冒险，会有真正的幸福，等待你去发现。

这种感觉，就像是小时候，我对星星许愿时的感觉似的。

永远不会忘记，你身体里的每一个原子，与经过十亿年形成一个星核的物质，是一样的。

你的身体里和身体外都有一个宇宙，等你去探索、去发现。

过程会很艰难。有实际价值的东西都来之不易。

牵着我的手吧。

感受它的悸动。

我和你一样地恐惧。

你不是一个人。

是的，你有你自己要走的路，而我有我自己要走的路。但幸运的是，至少在现在这一刻，你我的路是交织在一起的。

深深呼吸，把脚抬起来，向前迈。走出第一步。我们能够做到的。

我们一起前行。绘英语

Pretend You're Who You Want to Be

（文◎ Leo Babauta ）

Let's take a quick example: If I want to start running, to make running a daily habit, I think about runners I know or have read about. I read about their habits, their lifestyle, and imagine what it's like to be them. Then, I pretend I'm a runner myself. I think about what it's like to be a runner, how a runner would act, how a runner thinks and feels, what a runner's habits are.

I take the identity of a runner, and make it my own. Soon, I believe I'm a runner. And here's the magic: it becomes true! Just by pretending it, and assuming that identity, I become a runner. I think and act like one. And if I'm a runner, what do I do every day? I run.

This magical trick can work for any goal, and for any person. Imagine that you are that person, and you will be.

想象你就是你想成为的那个人

（文◎利奥·巴伯塔 译◎ Gesture）

让我来举个例子：如果我想开始跑步，并且养成每天跑步的习惯，我就会先思索一下我知道的或者是听说过的跑者。然后我会去了解他们的习惯和生活方式，并且想象一下成为他们后生活会是什么样子。接着，我假装我自己就是跑者，我会思考成为跑者会是什么样子，他会怎样跑，怎样思考，怎样感受，他的习惯又会是什么。

我扮演跑者的身份，并且让它成为我自己。很快，我相信我自己就是一位跑者。有魔性的是：这成了现实！仅仅是假装我是一位跑者，仅仅是假借跑者的身份，我就真的成了跑者。我想并且像一位跑者一样行动着。如果我是一位跑者，我每天会做什么呢？当然是跑！

这种魔性的技巧适用于任何目标以及任何人。想象你就是那个人，你就会成为那个人。

Stuff You Should know

一个正常人需要知道的几件小事

（文◎ Anonymous 佚名）

你可能会犯错，可并不意味着你是个失败的人。

不要害怕失败，你所走的每一步，都会让你离理想更近一些。

担心并不能阻止坏事情发生，只会耽误你享受美好。

别担心，一切都会好起来的。

失眠的时候，要放松、放松、放松，胡思乱想反而更睡不着。

有时候人们需要的不是建议，而仅仅是能有个人关心、倾诉。

偶尔给自己放个假，让忙碌的自己慢下来。

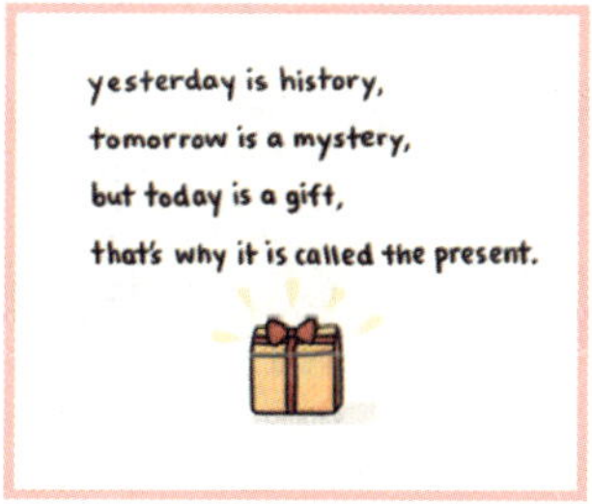

昨天已成历史，而明天是个谜团，只有今天是天赐的礼物。

生活总是很残酷，但却让你变得更坚强。

意林

告白的书

路渺且迢/有你就好

《那个神秘的宣愉小姐》

《余生，请对我好一点》

《冬夜有微光》

《绯色黎明》

《世界的另一个你》

《对方正在输入中》

《你是年少的欢喜，喜欢的少年是你》

《我不愿你一个人走过青春的荒芜》

《你是久爱、亦是心欢》

《从此晚安我自己》

《比心》

……